Acclaim for Katherine Min's *Secondhand World*

Finalist for the PEN/Bingham Prize

"Isa's adolescence unfolds in short chapters that read like impressionistic sketches . . . that resonate strongly in Min's quietly affecting novel."　　　　*—Entertainment Weekly*

"Min skillfully captures the angst and rebelliousness of this self-indulgent teen. . . . A remarkable achievement."　　　　*—Rocky Mountain News*

"This disquieting debut novel begins like a murder mystery: in a hospital burn unit, a badly scarred eighteen-year-old flatly informs us of her parents' death by fire. The story that follows, however, is less an investigation than an exorcism. . . . The writing is exquisite and exacting."　　*—The New Yorker*

"With a down-to-earth tone, Min sifts through the life of a torn and insecure girl from whom everyone can learn."　　　　*—New York Daily News*

"Min's spare prose not only vividly evokes this particular household . . . but resonates with the exquisiteness and oppressiveness of all family life."　　　　　　　　*—More*

"Katherine Min overturns conventional stereotypes in her portrayal of an Asian-American family."　　*—The Boston Globe*

Katherine Min

Secondhand World

Katherine Min was born in Champaign, Illinois, and was raised in Charlottesville, Virginia, and Clifton Park, New York. She attended Amherst College and the Columbia School of Journalism. She has been the recipient of writing grants from the National Endowment of the Arts and the New Hampshire Arts Council and is currently teaching at the University of North Carolina at Asheville.

www.katherinemin.com

Secondhand World

A NOVEL

Katherine Min

Anchor Books
A Division of Random House, Inc.
New York

FIRST ANCHOR BOOKS EDITION, FEBRUARY 2008

The Library of Congress has cataloged the Knopf edition as follows:
Min, Katherine.
Secondhand world: a novel / Katherine Min.—1st ed.
p. cm.
1. Korean Americans—Fiction. 2. Teenage girls—Fiction. 3. Parent and child—Fiction.
4. Domestic fiction. I. Title.
PS36131592S43 2006
813'.6—dc22   2006041038

Anchor ISBN: 978-0-307-27499-1

Book design by Soonyoung Kwon

www.anchorbooks.com

146122990

This book is dedicated to my parents,

Yungwha and Kongki Min,

for having the courage, the strength, and the vision
to succeed in this country, and for instilling in me
the sense that all things are possible.

Of all the tricks of memory, the cruelest
Is accuracy.

—GEOFFREY BROCK, "The Orpheus Variations,"
from *Weighing the Light*

Secondhand World

My name is Isadora Myung Hee Sohn and I am eighteen years old. I was recently ninety-five days in a pediatric burn unit at Tri-State Medical Center, in Albany, New York, being treated for second- and third-degree burns on my legs, complicated by a recurring bacterial infection. The same fire that injured me killed my parents, Hae Kyoung Chung and Tae Mun Sohn, on June 11, 1976, at approximately 3:20 a.m.

It's very isolating to recover from a severe burn injury. The pain requires a great deal of attention and inward focus. While your skin tissue rages and dies, you try and put yourself as far away as possible mentally, to take refuge in small, retrievable thoughts. Nursery rhymes are sometimes useful, as are television theme songs and knock-knock jokes.

. . .

Here's a riddle. A jumbo jet takes off from New York en route to Vancouver with 246 people on board. There's a massive snowstorm, visibility worsens, passengers pray and panic. The pilot loses control, and the plane ends up doing a nosedive on the border of the United States and Canada. The weather is so bad it takes the rescue helicopters two days to get to the remote crash site in the mountains. When they finally manage to land, amid the snow and the wreckage, they're confronted with a terrible dilemma. Since the plane crashed exactly on the boundary line separating the two countries, the recovering authorities don't know whether to bury the survivors in Canada or the United States.

It took me a while to get it. The trick is knowing where to focus. There's so much clamor and confusion—the plane, the storm, the panic—that you're easily thrown off. You end up overlooking what you should have noticed right away.

The fact is that survivors aren't buried. They keep walking around. They go through the varied motions of normalcy, trying to forget the screams, the shudder of the fuselage, the sound of crumpling metal. The frozen wait among the dead for rescue.

Celluloid

Many years before the fire that killed my parents, there was another fire. In Seoul, Korea, my mother had grown up among a harem of sisters, hoarded like treasure, quarantined like contagion, inside a high wall that contained the buildings and courtyards of the Chung family compound. My grandfather was a high-ranking government official who spent most of his time carousing with *kesang* girls and gambling at cards. My grandmother, herself the daughter of a high-ranking official, was terse and irritable, weighted by disappointment in birthing only girls.

One night when my mother was eleven, a treat was set up in the cramped building where the servants slept. It was the viewing of one of the first silent films from America, obtained somehow by my grandfather, along with an ancient projector that wheezed and smoked as it threw its jangled images upon the wall.

The room was hot and crowded, but my mother hardly noticed, so taken was she by the figures of the dancing women. They wore loose clothing that floated behind them as they danced, with emblematic jewelry, and makeup that emphasized their wide eyes and sensuous lips. Alabaster skin, marcelled hair piled high. My mother had never seen such women. Their serpentine sway—unaccompanied by music or sound of any kind, except the restless movement of the children and the hawking of the projector—was intricate, hypnotic. They were like Grecian goddesses come to life, like the sculpted caryatids my mother had once seen in a book in her father's library. She began to move along with them, in time to the unheard music. Her older sister Hae Ja pushed her away. "Hsst," she whispered, pinching her hard on the underside of the upper arm.

My mother huddled close to the projector. She watched as the strip of film wound around the metal spools in a tilting figure eight. Light from inside the machine streamed out toward the wall, thick with lolling dust. She looked up at the screen and then down to the projector again, trying to discover where they hid, these bright ladies, slender, swaying columns of pure grace. The old projector sputtered and paused and, before the audience had time to protest, the dancers disappeared in a spreading sepia bubble. Both film and projector burst into flames.

Children and servants began to scream as the room filled with smoke. My mother smelled something acrid and felt a strange prickling at the back of her neck. As the women had danced moments before, now the elderly *ajumma* who'd been attending the projector danced in spasmodic rhythm, a flume of fire blooming across her chest. The sensation at the back of my mother's neck became a searing pain. Her head was on fire and she fainted before she could push through, with the others, out of the room and into the dirt courtyard, where the adults ran with buckets of water.

An old servant saved her. He rushed inside the room and doused the fire nestled in her hair, carrying her out in his arms.

My grandmother, overwhelmed by daughters, disgraced by them, thought perhaps she would lose one that night, but my mother was not obliging. She survived with no major injury, just a spot, the size of a quarter, where her hair wouldn't grow, and a shiny purple scar, ropy and asymmetrical.

Two Names

After the accident my mother was declared unmarriageable and shipped off to a teachers college in Connecticut. She met my father the first week, at a party for Korean students in Hartford. Three months later she sent a picture home (my father in a trench coat over his best herringbone jacket), but my grandparents objected to the marriage. They had consulted an astrologer who claimed, given my parents' birth dates and the distance between the bottom of my father's nose and his top lip, that it was an inauspicious match.

They married anyway, and my mother dropped out of college to take dance lessons. In a photograph from those days she wore a black leotard with a pink tutu; she's bending down to tie the ribbons on her toe shoes, like a girl in a Degas painting.

She quit when she got pregnant. She told me this without resentment, but frequently enough so I understood that only maternal self-sacrifice had prevented her from a marvelous career. In playful moods, she would reenact the dance of the caryatid women as she remembered it, flowing like water, her arms a tossing sea, twisting and bending in a series of movements suggesting supplication, resistance, ardor, and grief.

Soon after I was born my parents had their first fight. My mother wanted to name me Isadora, after Isadora Duncan, the modern dancer. My father wanted to name me Myung Hee. I can imagine the way the discussion would go, my father's annoyance spiraling around my mother's cool determination, getting fettered in her obstinacy and confusing feminine allure.

"Isadora? Isadora?" I imagine my father saying, the word in his mouth like a bad taste. "What kind of Korean name is that?"

"No kind," my mother says, shrugging. "We're in America now."

"We're still Koreans," he says.

My mother doesn't answer. She smiles, beguiling him with her silence.

"I don't even know any Americans named Isadora," he grumbles.

"What Americans do you know?" my mother chides him. She pauses. "We could name her Ingrid," she says. "Or Ava. Or . . . Vivian."

"No, no," my father says, waving his hands in front of his face. "Please."

So I was named Isadora Myung Hee Sohn and called Isa by everyone but my father.

Apple Peel

My mother wore a wig to conceal her scar. It sat atop a Styrofoam head on her dresser, looking exactly like her real hair, thick and black, styled softly to just beneath the ears. To put it on she slipped both hands inside, fingers splayed as though she were winding yarn, and maneuvered it adroitly atop her head.

The procedure disturbed me, this half head of hair tugged on like a swim cap over my mother's own head, the naked Styrofoam left behind like a bald sentinel. I gouged a face in the Styrofoam with a ballpoint pen—nose like a lopsided *L,* kewpie lips, blank eyes the shape and size of pumpkin seeds.

My mother placed the wig atop my own head, where it sat like a long-haired lapdog. I looked at myself in the mirror. I was a strange-looking child, with a sallow complexion, my father's high forehead, and a large, crooked mouth. My mother laughed and called me "Beatle."

My mother. Her eyes, when she was happy, glanced across a room like sunlight, dark centers strewn with diamond facets. When she was unhappy, they seemed to retract beneath eyelids precisely outlined in liquid black, her look averted, cast down, all the giddy shine suddenly leached from the world.

For most of my life I watched her, ensorcelled by her beauty, by the daily acts of grace that were her movements. She peeled an apple by moving her thumb backward along the knife, her small hands seeming to float, to flutter, loosing the skin in one long ribbon, until it fell to the plate like a molted snakeskin. She raced down the aisles of the A & P, picking things up—red grapes, Camembert cheese, salmon steak—and tossing them in the grocery cart, as though she were on a TV game show. Tucking me in at night, she sang "Raindrops on Roses" or "Que Sera Sera," in perfect imitation of Doris Day. ". . . Will I be pretty? Will I be rich?" My mother would lean in, her breath hot in my ear. "Both, Isa," she would whisper. "You'll be both," and I'd feel a chill run through me at the maternal prophecy.

Nocturnal

If I watched my mother and was enthralled, I looked out for my father for different reasons. He was rarer in our house. For most of my childhood he would return to work after dinner, in pursuit of something called "tenure" that I did not understand but that seemed to hold talismanic power for both my parents. When he was home he was often irritable, snapping at me for biting my fingernails or spilling my milk. I tried not to attract his attention for this reason, though because he was mysterious, I was also drawn to him.

Nighttime was my father's dominion. I'd lie in bed and hear his slippered feet pass my door, pat-patting down the stairs. The door to the freezer would open and close, followed by the tinkling of ice in a glass, and I would picture my father sitting at our kitchen table in his pajamas, nursing a whiskey and water, attentive to the low hum of the refrigerator and the random headlights of passing cars. In the morning his glass would be sitting in the sink, empty except for an amber viscosity at the bottom, which I once swirled and sniffed and stuck my tongue into, recoiling at the burn. Sometimes a Korean magazine would be left on the table, its spine cracked open. My father's battered briefcase would be left on the floor, a yellow legal pad on top with strange characters marked in black—neither Korean nor English but numbers and Greek symbols in neat equations that ran the length of the paper.

These were my father's tracks, his spoor, which he left behind like some nocturnal animal. His insomnia, incurable and lifelong, reinforced the sense of his aloneness, his exile from a world in repose.

Incomprehension

When my father spoke to me in Korean, it was harsh, a vocabulary of scolding, of rebuke. *"Mae-majeulae?"* *Do you want a spanking?* uttered with a flat palm raised. *"Babo!"* *Stupid!* as we went over math problems together, his middle knuckle boring into my head as if to drill an answer into my skull.

In neither Korean nor English was my father voluble. The language of science was his mother tongue, the silver-voiced siren call to mathematical formulation. It was a language I had no ear for, its jargon so much gobbledygook. My father would grow frustrated as he tried to explain to me the second law of thermodynamics, or the concept of cold fusion. "Look," he would say, his hands raised in a gesture that was half threat and half entreaty, "it's not hard." And I'd try to follow him, his English as barbed as concertina wire, the concepts entering my head and leaving it unprocessed, like baggage down a conveyor belt.

Similarly, he failed at teaching me Korean. I remember lessons at the kitchen table, with colored wooden blocks and bowls of fruit. *"Sagwa-juseyo."* I would hand him an apple. *"Bae-juseyo."* I would hand him a pear. I would repeat the phrases after him in a dull, uninflected voice, and he would grow impatient at my lack of competence. "No, no, no. *Bbbb-ang!*" He would make an explosive sound with his lips. "Not *bang. Bbbb-ang* means bread. *Bang* is room! How many times do I have to tell you?"

When I was in eighth grade, he shipped me off to the basement of the Korean church. A self-proclaimed atheist and crusader against blind believing, my father had to turn to God to teach me his native language.

On Thursday afternoons, Michael Lee and Danny Kim played paper football across their desks, while I gossiped with Jenny and Eun Gyeong Lee about trampy Su Ok Min and her Hell's Angels boyfriend.

"Did they really do it?" I asked once, only to be met by the cold, mascara-clotted eye of Jenny Lee.

"Whaddya think?" she replied disdainfully. "The guy rides a Harley."

"An-nyeong!" Pastor Park would welcome us each week, with a hopeful expression that quickly turned desperate. *"Hanguk-mal halchul-arayo?"* Do you know how to speak Korean? And we would refuse to look at him, rolling our eyes and snapping our gum, muttering, *"Aaaa-niyo,"* sullenly under our breath. *No.*

After six weeks of this, Pastor Park abruptly ended classes. My father eventually gave up trying to teach me either of his two languages. It was my perception that he gave up on me altogether. I was too difficult, too rebellious, too unlike any Korean daughter he could possibly have imagined for himself. "Myung Hee-*ya*," he would say, "you should have been born a boy." And we would both think about Stephen and say nothing more, because it was true that I should have been, and because it was true that I was not.

Mr. Magoo

Our family photos burned in the fire—a thick maroon album stuffed with pictures, some inlaid in sticky corner holders, others loosely tucked in chronological piles. Black-and-white snapshots of my teenaged parents in their starched school uniforms; as a young couple, gawky in their affections (my father feeding my mother an ice cream cone); me in a high chair with a drooling smile; Stephen asleep in his stroller.

In my parents' wedding photo, they bent over a cake with four hands on a knife. My father wore a navy blue suit with a red carnation in his lapel; my mother's wedding dress was cocktail length, with a bell-shaped skirt and a short lace veil.

You could tell it was a Western wedding because my parents weren't wearing traditional Korean costume. You could tell because only Caucasians looked on in the background, a blond woman in a green dress with her hands up as though she'd been clapping, an older man with glasses who looked like one of my father's professors. You could tell because my parents were smiling, my father in that uneasy closed-mouth way he had, my mother more relaxed, genuine, showing her teeth inside the red coral of her lips.

According to Korean superstition, if a bride smiles, the firstborn will be a girl. Wedding portraits are mostly somber affairs, the woman with her head bowed, showing the straight middle part of her hair, and the groom with a serious expression, his own sober face serving as instruction for his wife. Of course, the assumption is that you wouldn't want to smile. Daughters you raise for another family, a Korean saying goes. Only sons remain your own.

I used to wonder at this photograph. How my father could've been so careless. My mother I understood, for she meant to break tradition, her smile like a thumb in the eye of expectation. She's triumphant in her white wedding gown—white, the Korean color of mourning—clutching the knife in both hands as though cleaving her way to the future. But my father, the orphan with the Sohn family name on the line, should have been more vigilant. Ordinarily so serious and cautious, how could he have failed to see—with those intent, piercing eyes—the tragic consequences of that one shy smile?

Over a period of about five years—from the time I was two to the time I was seven—my mother had a series of miscarriages. Each episode left her rattled and weak, and my father was forced to take charge of my welfare while she recuperated in bed. These were among the best times I can remember spending with him. For dinner he would make Sapporo Ichiban ramen noodles, which he bought in cases from an Asian grocery store in New Haven, sometimes adding garish pink slices of *kamaboko*, Japanese fish cake, and crunchy yellow *takwang* pickle. My favorite was a version with a beaten egg dropped in the broth, its eggy yellow tendrils fixing from viscous liquid, like a magic trick.

After dinner we'd sit on the hideous green-striped couch, a hand-me-down from my father's thesis advisor. My father would bring out his pipe and fuss with the paraphernalia of tobacco and matches, the result of which would be a pleasant piney smell, like a campfire, that I came to identify with him long after he'd quit the pipe for good.

Sometimes he would listen to me read books aloud, *Animal Riddles* and *Hop on Pop*. Once when I was seven, I read him the first paragraph of a *Time* magazine article about a microscopic parasite that lived in human eyelashes. He was so impressed that he took his pipe out of his mouth and told me to go on.

At night he'd turn on the black-and-white television set. Reception was poor, and the two stations we got came in on a slant, stretched to the left and quivering slightly; Walter Cronkite was accompanied by a gray penumbra that vibrated behind his head like some carnivorous shadow. It was wartime, the casualty count kept like a sports score in a running tally at the top of the screen—images of soldiers in the jungle, their dog tags settled against hairless chests, eyes empty, helmets like tortoise shells. Riveted, my father sat, chomping on the stem of his pipe, shifting it from one side of his mouth to the other. Occasionally something he saw would cause him to shake his head and make a violent clucking noise of shame or disbelief, and his pipe would fall to his lap with a spray of sparks.

If I tried to get his attention during the news, he'd shush me, holding up a hand in warning. "Don't interrupt, Myung Hee," he'd say to me. "It is war."

When I was seven, my mother became pregnant again, and this time they were confident enough to tell me. A brother on the way, my father told me. Or sister, my mother said, though she, too, wished for a boy, to please my father and to one-up her mother, who'd produced nothing but girls.

And a boy it was. My brother, Stephen Myung Hwan Sohn, born two weeks prematurely, at only five pounds. Jaundiced from birth, he had to stay in the hospital for a week, basking under special heat lamps like a tiny sunbather.

I went to the hospital with my father and looked in the nursery window. My father tapped the glass as a nurse held Stephen up. Wrapped in flannel, with a knit cap on his head, my brother squinted, fists balled and flailing. My father made clucking noises with his tongue on the roof of his mouth. I thought Stephen looked like Mr. Magoo, the blind old man in the cartoon, but when I told my father, he did not laugh.

"This is your brother," he said, looking not at me but into the window. He said it sternly, as though I'd called him ugly. My father continued to tap the glass and cluck, and the expression on his face, repeated in his reflection, was rapt, like a window-shopper gazing in at some glittering object he has no means to pay for.

In between my father and the window, I waved too, but I was aggrieved. My brother's face was mottled from crying and yellow with jaundice, his eyes screwed up like knotholes, mouth agape. He was cranky and funny-looking, and I felt no kinship to him. Behind me, my father tapped and cooed with a tenderness that made him strange to me. I pressed my forehead to the cool glass and closed my eyes.

Isatree

Whatever my initial impressions, I soon learned to adore my brother. I pushed his carriage proudly down the sidewalk, my mother beside me with a wary hand outstretched. He was an exuberant baby, sloe-eyed and fat, with red, round cheeks and a gummy grin. He wore a white bonnet with eyelet lace, which my mother had ordered from a Sears catalog, and a pastel blue terry-cloth jumpsuit with snaps down the front, a picture of a lamb or bunny sewn on the chest.

Strangers would beam down at Stephen and I would stand over him like a carny barker, demonstrating how he could grip my finger so tightly, how he could coo and gurgle, how his sturdy little legs could bicycle in the air with delight. *Amazing baby! Step right up, step right this way!"*

My father accepted a job at the state university in Albany when I was nine and Stephen was almost two, and we moved from our tiny Connecticut apartment to a suburb in upstate New York. The houses in our development were ranches or colonials, with blue or white aluminum siding and a bit of brick around the front doors.

Ours was the only split-level, made of gray clapboard, with a long roof slanting to one side. It was a modern-looking house, with large picture windows and a living room that occupied the entire middle story. Although the other houses sat in cleared lots with a tree or two in the front yard, ringed by geraniums or marigolds, our house was surrounded by trees—two fat oaks in front that must have been hundreds of years old, two maples at the back that sawed at our roof and bedroom windows when it was windy.

My mother loved that we had our own yard, a third of an acre with a stand of white birch in the back. It was there that my brother learned to walk, toddling unsteadily from the front of the house to the back, in the mud brown corrective shoes he had to wear. My mother would sunbathe on a green plaid lawn chair, her already bronze limbs turning a darker, more velvety brown, pale sides of her arms upturned, her face cocked slightly backward.

"Isa," she'd say, out of the corner of her mouth, "watch your brother. Make sure he doesn't go out in the road."

There was almost no traffic, but I would chase Stephen across the lawn, picking him up by the straps of his overalls and swinging him to a halt. We would race Matchbox cars down the gentle slope of our driveway, dodging acorns and bits of twig that the oaks constantly shed. Stephen ran to retrieve the cars at the bottom and brought them back, loudly proclaiming his victory.

During a fifth-grade field trip to a tree nursery, we were each given a small pine to take home and plant. Stephen used his plastic beach shovel to help me dig a hole on the side of our yard. I used a metal spade, supervised by my father, who knew nothing about gardening but much about dangerous instruments in the hands of children. I was proud of the little tree that I plopped into that hole, tamping down the loose soil like I was tucking it in bed.

We didn't realize that I'd planted it over the septic system, but the tree grew impressively in the next five years, straight up, with no branches except the two it started with, a telephone pole with a pair of straggly arms.

"Isatree," Stephen called it. Isatree—all one word. For years it was home base for our tag and hide-and-seek games, the bark worn smooth at the spots where our hands would touch it. I got pine pitch in my hair once from leaning against it, and my mother had to cut the tangle out with scissors while I cried.

I see Stephen underneath Isatree, much too short to reach the first branch, his hands in front of his face. He's grinning, peeking out from his fingers to see if I'm coming. Of course I pretend I can't find him, pacing the lawn, loudly lamenting, "Where's Stephen? Where could he be?" until, unable to stand it anymore, my brother drops his hands and comes running toward me.

"Here I am, here I am, Ee-see," he says.

Chink

"Hey, Chink. Chinky Chink Chink."

"Gook girl, why don't you go home where you belong?"

"Yeah, gookland. Go back to gookland."

I sit closest to the window on the bus seat, perfectly rigid, unmoving. Next to me Jenny Going is sure not to let her shoulder or knee touch mine.

We pull up to the entrance of the school. Outside, the bus monitors cross their arms against the chill as kids spill from buses like misshapen beads and scatter along the sidewalk.

"What's the matter, gook?"

"What's the matter, Chinee?"

I feel the heat in my face, blasting like a furnace. The bus slows to a halt, and we wait suspended until we hear the sigh of the brakes and the squeak of hinges as the door folds open. I stand up. Something like a SuperBall is bouncing around inside my chest, winging from my heart to my rib cage. I turn toward the boys—Roger Huckins, Tom Kerry, Paul Weaver and his brother, Jimmy—and I say, infusing my voice with a contempt I do not feel, "For your information, I'm Korean!"

A look of confusion clouds their faces. "What's that?" says Roger Huckins.

I had not counted on this further question. "It's, like, a totally different country," I say, following Jenny up the aisle in a haughty show of superior knowledge.

I walk quickly toward the main entrance. Someone jostles me running past. My next step meets resistance, and the next thing I know I am falling through the air. My books and lunch box go flying, and I land on both knees on frozen asphalt.

"That still makes you a gook," I hear Tom Kerry say as he walks away.

"You tell those boys," my father says, pointing with his chop-sticks at me from across the kitchen table. "You tell them Korean civilization is five thousand years old. America not even born yet, still belong to Indians and wild animals."

"Dad!"

My father's eyes grow wide at my look of skepticism. "Admiral Yi invented ironclad battleships, hundreds of years before the Spanish Armada. Koreans invented printing press two hundred years before Gutenberg! You tell them—"

"*Yeobo,*" my mother says. She taps her rice paddle on my father's plate, dislodging another serving. "*Geurojima!*" *Cut it out.*

"No!" my father says, still looking at me. "Isa needs to have pride in being Korean. She needs to educate these boys. What do they know about us? Nothing. They think Chinese, Vietnamese, Korean all the same. Stupid!"

"I tried, Dad," I say. Though he is angry at the boys, he is yelling at me. My ignorance has contributed in some way to their ignorance; my lack of defense against attack is proof of my own dubious allegiance. "They don't care about printing presses. They don't care about ironclad boats."

My father's eyes narrow. "You make them care, Myung Hee," he says.

I imagine describing Admiral Yi's turtle boat to Tom Kerry, the ingenuity of its design—a craft light enough to skim the ocean, yet cast in iron to ward off enemy weaponry. I imagine explaining the significance of the Gutenberg Bible, the preemptive brilliance of the Korean minds that engineered moveable type.

I picture Tom's jaw dropping in admiration. "I'm sorry," he says. "I thought you were just a dumb gook."

I give my father a sideways look. His chopsticks are still thrust in my direction. "Right, Dad," I say, wasting my sarcasm in the face of his righteousness. "Whatever you say."

Acquire

My parents were fast on their way to gaining the American dream: a steady, good-paying job; a car that ran; one child of each gender; a nice suburban house with a two-car garage and a bit of yard to tend and mow.

Christmases became a slugfest of torn wrapping paper and stick-on bows from which emerged board games, toy trains, Farberware, teddy bears, vinyl records, Fair Isle sweaters, and once—from my father to my mother—a rabbit-skin coat. I owned a red Schwinn three-speed bike. My father had a set of Titleist golf clubs in a sleek leather bag. Stephen had a jungle gym in the backyard with its own swing, teeter-totter, and plastic slide. And my mother, who presided over all purchases with girlish wonder, had a rose floral couch with matching wing chairs, a Zenith television, and wall-to-wall carpeting in beige.

One of my mother's favorite objects was a merry-go-round of gold angels that she placed on the coffee table every Christmas. When she lit the candles, the angels would orbit a gold pole in the middle, which was stamped with five-pointed stars. I used to sit between the Christmas tree and the table, watching the angels spin, fascinated by the motion that seemed to be caused by the heat. My father tried to explain the physics to me once, but I preferred the incomprehensible mystery.

For a few months in 1970 my mother's consumer dreams settled on an avocado green Whirlpool dishwasher with automatic settings. We'd never owned a dishwasher. I was almost twelve, but I was never asked to do more than clear the table or dry, while my mother donned yellow Playtex gloves and attacked the dishes with sudsy water and Brillo.

She took us to an appliance store one day, driving the new Dodge that we'd bought five months before. My mother dressed up when she went out, and now she checked her coral lipstick in the rearview mirror, adjusted a clip-on earring, and smoothed a hand down the back of her wig.

"Let's go eye-shop," she said, as we pulled into the parking lot. That's what she called window-shopping, though she seldom just looked. Stephen and I were used to these jaunts, and, though we couldn't have cared less about appliances, furniture, or women's clothing, we were easily swayed by her enthusiasms.

Inside the store, Stephen and I played hide-and-seek up and

down the corridors of refrigerators and washer/dryers. I snuck from row to row, a little anxious when I didn't immediately discover my brother's blue plaid shirt and shiny black hair, but he always reappeared eventually, crawling out from behind an oven or a freezer, running to find me, his mouth wide in the ecstasy of our reunion.

We returned to our mother's side in time to watch her commune with the display dishwashers, listening to the fervent sales pitch of a man with a black mustache.

"This one is your most ee-conomical model," he said, spreading his hands proudly atop a dishwasher as though it were a prize heifer. My mother stroked its glossed surface with her delicate fingers, pulled down the door to reveal the plastic racks where the dishes would go, lifted the removable basket for cutlery. She opened the top drawer, where inverted glasses could be placed in martial lines atop rubberized prongs. She pushed the drawer back in, closed the dishwasher, and fiddled with the dials and buttons. NORMAL WASH. POTS AND PANS. QUICK RINSE.

My mother touched that dishwasher as though it were a good-luck charm, a rabbit's foot or a four-leaf clover. Her fingers left its surface with great reluctance, settling finally on the metal clasp of her handbag.

"You can't go wrong with this par-ticular model," the salesman said, smiling. "It's got revolutionary technology!"

"Y-yes, I see," my mother said. English on her lips came out trippingly, with a sibilant charm that made it seem less accent than affectation.

On the drive home, my mother's eyes were obsidian-bright.

When she'd told the salesman that she had to go home and consult her husband, he had winked at her. "Can't imagine any man could deny such a pretty wife anything," he'd said, and my mother had blushed.

That night she washed the dishes with a vengeance, in triple time, and I tried to keep up with her, drying them with a red-striped towel. My father sat at the kitchen table coaxing Stephen to finish his dinner.

"*Aigo, yeobo,*" my mother said. She peeled off her gloves and started rubbing the backs of her elbows. "So tired. Too much washing!"

My father hardly looked up. He just nodded and opened his own mouth slightly as he urged Stephen to take a bite of peas.

My mother tried again. She sighed, blew some hair out of her eyes. "Automatic dishwasher would save so much time," she said. "So convenient."

My father didn't seem to hear.

"Don't you think automatic dishwasher would be more convenient?" my mother persisted. "Tae Mun!"

My father finally looked up. "*Wae-geurae?*" he said sharply. *What's the matter?*

My mother regarded him for a moment, then wheeled around and threw the rubber gloves at his chest. "You do it!" she said, stomping out of the room with a strangled cry.

Stephen stared with his mouth open, a half-chewed pea hanging from his bottom teeth. I continued to rub the plate in my hand with the towel. My father sprang up, and I heard his footsteps bound up the stairs and the bedroom door slam. We could hear their voices, my father's deep and in Korean only, my mother's shrill, mixing Korean and English. "You don't care," my mother sobbed. "You don't care!"

I listened for a while longer, tense and silent. Stephen, though he was only four, listened also. Because my parents fought mostly in Korean, we couldn't follow what was said, but we learned to listen for the waves of sound breaking upon each other, pitching toward crescendo, then falling, shrinking, finally slipping into a silence that was not exactly peace, but respite.

I put Stephen to bed, reading him a chapter of Paddington. It was his favorite; he'd taken to asking for marmalade sandwiches and saying he was from Peru. I wasn't paying much attention to what I was reading, straining as I was to hear what was going on in our parents' bedroom.

"Why is Mommy sad?" Stephen asked, after my reading had slowed to a stop.

"'Cause she wants a dishwasher," I said.

"Like the one in the store?"

"Yes."

My brother considered. My parents' voices were muffled now, murmurs behind the wall. "I want one, too, Isa," he said. "Don't you?"

"Shh, go to sleep now," I said. I heard the bedroom door opening. I tucked the covers in around Stephen, kissed him good night, and went back downstairs. My mother was alone in the kitchen. When she turned to smile at me, she was flushed and puffy-eyed.

"Got your brother to bed?"

I nodded.

"Thank you, Isa," she said. "Oh, Isa, your father said yes! We're going to get a dishwasher! On layaway plan!" She did a little pirouette in her slippered feet, took my hand and twirled beneath it.

"Great!" I said, though I didn't know what a layaway plan was.

She laughed and leaned toward me, tears in her eyes. "I have to teach you," she whispered. "Something every woman should know—how to get man to give in. Even difficult man like your father!" She threw her head back and laughed until I could see the fillings in the back of her mouth. The salesman had been right—who could deny her anything? I picked up the dish towel, and we worked together until all the dishes were washed and dried.

"Not much longer," my mother vowed, "and I'll never have to wash dishes by hand again!"

Delivery

Three weeks after my mother's triumph over my father, two men in a van came to deliver our new dishwasher. Seventh grade had started for me a month earlier; it was the end of October and the days were getting shorter, with the premonition of winter in the clear air of late afternoons.

We were studying insects in science class. We each had a killing jar containing cotton balls saturated with ammonia, and we got to roam the woods beyond the school grounds looking for specimens. I had two ants, some kind of beetle that I'd captured in the corner of the cafeteria doorway, and a green spider that Mrs. Cranston said wasn't an insect. Theresa Graves and I had been lifting up logs and uncovering crawling loot—mostly ants and grubs. She got mad when I let go too soon and scraped her hand.

"Isa, you need to be more careful," Mrs. Cranston said. "Theresa, you may go in and see the nurse."

Mrs. Cranston had it in for me. I'd forgotten to turn in a worksheet at the beginning of the year and she was always complaining that my handwriting was sloppy, but I knew the real reason she didn't like me. She'd told me that her daughter-in-law was Korean, and she hadn't sounded pleased.

"My son's over there now," she'd said, looking at me as though I were responsible. "In the army. That's how they met."

And once when we were dissecting fetal pigs, she'd come over to me and said, "You people eat things like this over there, don't you?"

After Theresa had gone to the nurse's office, I sat down on a log. I put the jar up to my face and watched an unidentified green bug—an aphid?—stagger drunkenly across the poison cotton bed. It seemed cruel what we were doing, killing insects and mounting them on pins in the name of science. Still, there was something compelling in the cruelty; I had never before watched a thing die.

The bug fell over on its back and wiggled its legs in the air. It looked slapstick, like a Charlie Chaplin routine. One moment I was watching it, the next I felt a stab of fear. My head snapped back. It was like the bracing ammonia shock to attention, as if the boundary line that separated me from the bug inside the glass had momentarily dissolved, and all our atoms had slopped together before reassembling in their proper configurations.

I unscrewed the top of the jar and dumped the bug out. It was too late; he lay motionless on the ground. Still the fear did not abate. I was panicked; I was either going to pass out or get sick. My impulse was to run away from the woods, to keep running and running until I'd outdistanced the terror. I tried to stand but my legs gave way.

Some of my classmates noticed me squatting on the ground, the contents of my killing jar scattered around me. I was shaking. Someone told Mrs. Cranston and she came over. "What's going on here, Isa?" she said. "What have you done?"

I slumped to the ground, sobbing, my whole body shivering uncontrollably among the dirt and leaves, while my stunned teacher and classmates looked on.

I spent the rest of the afternoon in the nurse's office, lying on a cot with my teeth chattering. I had no temperature, and the nurse, Miss Verrill, could find nothing the matter with me.

"Killing insects can disturb a child with a sensitive disposition," Miss Verrill told Mrs. Cranston.

"They're bugs," Mrs. Cranston said. "She's just being hysterical."

They tried calling my mother to pick me up, but there was no answer, so they sent me home on the bus as usual. I felt a bit better by then, a little weak and shivery but not violently so. I sat toward the front with my face pressed against the bus window, looking out at the passing landscape; the white line on the side of the road; the half-barren, half-bright trees in red and orange; the houses with raked front lawns, children hurrying inside with their satchels and lunch boxes. I thought if I could catalog everything I saw and identify it correctly, I'd be all right, leaping from item to item as though they were stepping-stones across danger- ously swift water. Tree. House. People.

"Hey, Chinky, whatsamatter? You got ants in your pants?" Paul Weaver yelled from the back of the bus.

"Yeah, you swallow Chinese jumping beans or what?" said Tom Kerry. "Was that supposed to be some kinda sneaky Viet- cong trick?"

I closed my eyes. I could hear the kids around me snickering.

"Spaz! She's such a spaz! She was having a spaz attack!"

"See her eat dirt?"

"Gooks gotta eat dirt; otherwise they starve."

"And bugs, too. She probably got sick from eating too many bugs!"

It was the first time the bus bullies had picked on me this year. Until now they had chosen to concentrate their attentions on a shy, delicate boy named Bobby Silski. With my eyes closed I could see their faces—pale and freckled, pink-cheeked and pinched, with hair the color of wheat or barley; their eyes big and blue, narrowed and greenish. There were no black faces, no faces of the Iroquois or Mohawk that we had studied in sixth grade; no brown faces like the ones in my report on the country of Honduras; and there were no faces like the ones I saw on the news at night, the ones in the sloping hats with their loose cloth- ing, expressionless on the receiving end of guns and cameras— the faces that looked most like mine.

A sharp feeling of nausea rose in me, which was only partly the nausea of the bus in motion and the closed-in smell of sweat and breath. If I didn't open my eyes, I'd be fine, I thought. If I could just lean forever against the glass, my forehead glued along the smooth surface.

Something was wrong with me. I was terribly sick. It seemed natural to me somehow that Mrs. Cranston and the kids on the bus could tell that this was so—could see it in the slant of my eyes and the sallowness of my skin. The illness I felt in my gut was only an inward sign of an external strangeness. It wasn't a secret that could be hidden; it was on the surface. All you had to do was look. "One of these things is not like the others," they sang on *Sesame Street,* which Stephen watched every afternoon. And it was evident that I was that unlike thing, the forever Other. Triangle among circles. Apple among pears.

It was the beginning of the realization that I did not belong, like the cowbird's egg hatched in the robin's nest. How strange that it should come on this particular afternoon, with my head spinning and my heart rattling inside my chest. It was an unmooring, my sense of self adrift, and though I couldn't have articulated it at the time, I felt such a devastating sense of loneliness that I knew it would never entirely leave me. I felt I was, in some permanent, unconditional way, alone.

As I got off the bus, my knees almost buckled beneath me.

"You okay?" asked Rudy, the bus driver.

I managed a nod.

"Take it easy now," he called after me.

I walked slowly toward my house, ignoring the knocking on the bus windows, the muffled laughter and pointing fingers. I felt like an old woman, stooped and aching, leaden feet shuffling unsteadily through dead leaves.

I wasn't surprised when Mrs. Williamson, our next-door

neighbor, met me at my front door. After the trauma of the afternoon, nothing would have seemed strange to me. Even as she gathered me to her bosom and wept, I couldn't process anything beyond my own emptiness and fear. She smelled like cake, powdery and sweet, and I wept right along with her. We cried that way for a while, wrapped in each other's arms, as though we always greeted one another this way, as though our relationship were predicated on more than a few dozen words shouted across driveways and a jaunty wave of a hand out the car window.

I don't remember what words Mrs. Williamson used, when she finally did use words. I don't remember much more of that day, or the days that followed. It was as if the attack I'd had in the woods had precipitated some kind of fugue state. I felt as though I were moving through syrup, as if time had simultaneously slowed and sped up, and I was another organism entirely, pushing up from the earth to full grown in mere seconds.

The deliverymen had come to install my mother's dishwasher that afternoon. They demonstrated the whole procedure for her—the way you loaded the soap in the little tray and pushed it closed on its spring-loaded jaws, the way you could select from various options, hot water or cold rinse, regular or heavy-duty wash.

Stephen wasn't at nursery school that day because he was getting over a cold, but after lunch he'd felt so much better that my mother had shooed him out into the front yard. (He wasn't allowed to go past the low hedge in the front of the house, or beyond the big maple to the right, or Isatree to the left.) He was gathering acorns and twigs to set up obstacle courses for his Matchbox cars.

The only place the cars would glide was on the driveway. I'd spent countless hours out there with him, conducting races with five or six cars at once, starting them at the part of the pavement with the steepest grade and letting them cruise to the finish line about four feet away. Stephen had a favorite car—purple with orange interior—that almost always won. He liked it best, not because it was fast but because he said it was lucky.

The deliverymen, having finished the job they were hired to do, got back into their van. Perhaps they were late for their next delivery; perhaps it was time for an afternoon break. In any case, they backed out in a hurry. They didn't see my brother squatting just behind them, racing his tiny cars down the smoothly tarred slope.

My mother stood at the window above the kitchen sink, looking out onto the side of the driveway. She saw the van, the men inside it; she scanned the yard but could not find Stephen. It would've taken a moment to process. She saw my brother's toy cars whizzing down the driveway, and Stephen crouched a foot away from the van's right tire. She screamed and screamed. She banged on the window so hard she went right through it, fracturing a bone on the side of her hand. By the time she ran out the door, it was too late. Stephen's body was lying on the driveway, and the workmen were getting out of the van confused, thinking they'd caught a tree branch. My mother knelt beside her son, took his head in her lap, while the deliverymen ran inside for a phone.

Passage

My father would always say that there were sixty seconds in a minute, sixty minutes in an hour, twenty-four hours in a day. He used to say this in response to my complaints that a car trip was too long, when I was impatient to go to a friend's house, or if I'd been promised a treat. "Sixty seconds in a minute," he'd say. "No more, no less."

And though he was, as usual, entirely accurate, I was irritated by the way he could completely discount the experience of time passing, which was fitful and malingering. A moment elongated to filament like saltwater taffy, sped up and fell over itself like a strobe-light sequence in a silent movie. I resented the way he tried to make everything seem simpler than it was, adhering to facts when facts were so clearly beside the point.

For about three years after Stephen's death, my sense of time was skewed both ways—individual moments seeming to come to a standstill, a whole year disappearing into ether. What is left are snapshots, pinpoints of illumination against a background of darkness.

Moment: I sit in a wooden pew, in a black dress with a lace collar, listening to Pastor Park talk about Stephen. His thin lips draw up against an uncertain smile. He speaks about our family's terrible misfortune, my brother's innocence, the mercy of God, as though he were speaking of the weather, or of the ivory-colored Cadillac he drives to and from church.

"He's gone to a better place," he says in English, and then in Korean, and I stare at the white coffin with the lilies on top and think of how Stephen would've hated that small space, the still-ness and the dark. My mother is still in the hospital. I wonder what she's doing there on the day that her son is being eulogized. In my hand is Paddington Bear. I'd planned to give it to the undertaker to place beside Stephen in the casket, but for some reason I haven't, and it's still here, its floppy yellow hat and scruffy fur mashed against the hem of my dress.

Moment: A neighbor comes by with a homemade casserole. Mrs. Williamson has them on a rolling schedule. I can't remember if it's Mrs. Sanderson or Mrs. Benoit—the one with the stiff gray upsweep of hair and orange makeup like a mask. It's clear she's feeling uncomfortable and doesn't want to stay. My mother's upstairs sleeping and my father's at work. "The directions are right on there, hon. Just heat the oven to three seventy-five and put it in for forty-five minutes. Take the foil off the last ten. I'll come back for my pan."

She turns back toward the door.

"My mother broke her hand," I say. "Banging on the window."

The woman's face freezes. She twitches to arrange it back inside her orange mask. "Sweetheart, I'm so sorry. It's a terrible tragedy. Terrible. But you know God's going to take good care of your brother up in heaven, don't you? He's a little angel now." She looks at me hopefully.

"Want to play Parcheesi?" I ask her.

Moment: My mother's head bent over a card table in the living room. On the table, a jigsaw puzzle. She sits with her back to me, in her blue terry-cloth robe, fingering a piece in her delicate hands as though it were a jewel. The puzzle has thousands of pieces, with geometric patterns and repeating colors: three different shades of red, four different textures of green; sky indistinguishable from ocean; bird beaks facing right, bird beaks facing left. She isn't wearing her wig, and I am startled by the purple scar at the back of her head, like the wounded eye of a Cyclops. As I get closer, she turns and smiles, but it's a muscular exercise only, a ghost gesture, the remembrance of smiling. The tears in her eyes seem permanently lodged there, like tiny embedded diamonds.

She goes back to the hospital three times that year. Each time my father explains that she needs more rest. She returns red-eyed and flinching, her back and shoulders hunched like a crone's.

One day I come home from school to find her in Stephen's room cutting up his OshKosh overalls with oversized pinking shears. "What are you doing?" I ask.

"Oh, Isa, making rags," she says, her face flushed with exertion. She raises the scissors toward me, and for a moment I am frightened. I take a step back. "Otherwise, what's the use?" she says, getting back to work.

I begin to feel like a girl in a fairy story. Around our split-level, a tangle of briars rises up, thorny and thick, my mother dwelling in enchanted sleep, the king distracted. And the princess in the tower, growing her hair, dreaming of escape.

I think my parents believed that the nature of Stephen's death exposed them for the careless foreigners they were, unable to keep their young from harm in this complex country of dishwashers and delivery vans. I think they felt it set them apart. Even as my mother got better and things returned to an approximation of normal, this pervading sense of separation remained. My mother had no real friends; she seldom went out. My father worked too hard and stayed at the office too long. I didn't bring friends home—not because it was explicitly forbidden but because I couldn't see them there, in that space that housed my parents' grief, couldn't imagine what we would do surrounded by the strange smells of *kimchi* and fish *chig'ge,* among the celadon vases and hanging scrolls of Chinese poetry in feathered black brushstrokes.

Eventually my mother returned to putting on her wig and getting dressed each day, making out grocery lists and cooking my favorite dishes. My father started coming home to eat the meals, scolding me for spilling my milk, demanding to check my math homework. But my brother, by his absence, remained the strongest presence in our house. Even as my parents spoke to me in the old familiar ways, I could feel their distraction. I began to feel insubstantial, a transparency that hung like a scrim between them and the child they had lost. It was in the monotone of their voices as they talked to me without listening to themselves, in the momentary confusion as they scanned my face for features that weren't there.

Even at the height of her recovery, my mother never used the avocado dishwasher that had been her most fevered consumer dream. She continued to wash our dishes by hand, in yellow Playtex gloves, with an extravagance of soapy water. My father, raking leaves in the backyard, would stand beside the swing set he'd never dismantled, sometimes sitting gingerly on one side of the teeter-totter, as though waiting for Stephen to take his place on the other side.

I'd stare at the photograph of my parents' wedding and feel the weight of my mother's hope like a medicine ball to the chest. Why had she smiled? It was so clearly a son they should have secured for their firstborn. Stephen Myung Hwan Sohn. Son and heir. They didn't have to tell me. Somehow I just knew, knew in the way that children know. Who is loved and who is merely borne.

Proof

My father wore a green badge clipped to the pocket of his lab coat. To measure radioactivity, he told me, something you couldn't see or smell, but that could make you sick. It had a small photo on the front and looked like a regular ID card, except thicker. I liked to clip it to my collar and pretend I was a grown-up with a dangerous job, some glamorous, dimly understood version of my father's. I imagined the green badge suddenly glowing red, the invisible something that could make you sick overflowing its small boundary, the concerned faces of doctors blurring in and out of focus as I fell stricken to the floor.

Though I had a few friends around the neighborhood, I spent most of my time before Stephen was born alone, reading, writing an episodic novel about an Englishwoman who had seventeen children, and inventing games that revolved around giant pipe cleaners, stuffed animals, and a collapsible wooden laundry rack.

On Sunday mornings I wandered through the neighborhood, knowing that all my friends were in church. Ginny Townsend's mother had invited me to go, and I wanted to very much. Church seemed like a club everyone belonged to except me. I imagined something important happening there, exclusionary rites of goodness and celebration.

"Ignorance and fear," my father said. "That's why people need religion. They're afraid of the unknown." My father sat up straight, his expression making it clear that *he* was not afraid.

"Why?" I asked.

My father shrugged. "They're afraid of death, what comes after life. They cannot imagine it. So they make up things."

"Is that why we don't go to church?"

"Ye-es," my father said uncertainly. He glanced at the kitchen where my mother had her back turned, stirring spaghetti sauce on the stove. "Your mother is Buddhist," he said. "But Buddhism is not really a religion, more like philosophy."

"They believe in reincarnation. Mom says if I don't behave, I'll come back as a bug."

My father chuckled. "I don't know about that," he said.

He seldom spoke to me so expansively, conversing almost as though I were an adult, and I was determined to engage him for as long as possible.

"What are *you?*" I asked.

He pursed his lips and scratched the corner of one eye, just under his glasses. "I am a scientist, Myung Hee," he said, "and scientists require evidence. They observe and record what they see. In science, we look for proof. When I die, I will find out. If there is a God, I will see with my own eyes."

"Ginny's mom says God exists."

"How does she know?"

"Because . . ." I hesitated. "Because she believes it."

My father looked triumphant. "Belief and knowledge," he said. "Completely different."

The night Stephen died, I woke to the sound of my father's footsteps on the stairs. I listened to the freezer door open and shut, and ice cubes rattle against glass. Lying in bed, I pictured him sitting at the table in his pajamas, cradling the whiskey to his chest. Before I went downstairs, I slipped into Stephen's room and glanced at the bed. His stuffed animals crouched on their haunches in the dark; a scattering of books lay across the floor. The only thing missing was the small shape of the boy in the bed, his tousled black hair on the pillow with the race cars, a bare heel peeking out from the tangle of blue bedcovers.

Stephen was in heaven, Mrs. Williamson had told me earlier that day, though it already seemed years ago. Heaven. For some reason I had an image of a doctor's waiting room crammed with old people reading magazines, staring at brown carpet. I saw Stephen in the corner, where the children's toys were kept—the Fisher-Price farm, the wooden balls strung on metal wires, the colored plastic rings that were chewed at the edges.

In the kitchen my father sat almost exactly as I had imagined him. He did not lift his head as I came into the room.

"Where's Mom?" I asked in a voice higher than my own.

"In the hospital," he said. "Her hand."

"Is it broken?"

"Yes."

"Dad?"

"Yes?"

"Do you think Stephen is in heaven?"

I watched as my father took a sip of his drink and put the glass down very deliberately on the table. He put his hand to his eyes and rubbed the lids.

"Myung Hee," he said wearily, "I don't know. Maybe . . . maybe he is. Why not?"

He was not in the least convincing. His voice could not conceal his impatience, but in his eyes, when he released them from beneath his hand, there was something I had never seen before—a look of uncertainty, of blinding loss—that conveyed to me, simultaneously and profoundly, his skepticism and his longing.

Fluency

Around the time Stephen died I started reading the dictionary. I read it like a novel, page by page, not for the express purpose of memorizing words and definitions, but for the feel of words rolling around in my head, like those air-blown balls featured in the Pick 4 lottery game that came on before the news. They seemed to float in my brain, words—lovely and sinuous, devious and clever—surprising me with their specificity, their shadings, and their oddness. I would underline the words I didn't know, in *Jane Eyre* or *The Scarlet Letter*, saving them to look up all at once in a feeding frenzy of new vocabulary. I began to put certain words I loved on three-by-five cards, with their definitions on the back; words like "calliope" and "meager," "tergiversate" and "lacuna."

My father was initially excited by my virtuosity, but despite the fact that my grades in English were consistently my highest, I didn't always score well on individual papers or literature exams.

"Why did you get B on this paper?" my father would demand, going over my assignments. "You're always reading."

I'd shrug, unable to explain that it was not for sharing, this passion of mine, not for pandering to teachers or showing off. It was something I did for myself, hoarding words like "cat's-eye marbles," "Indian-head nickels," or other such childhood treasure.

It was fluency I was after, and it was enough that I possessed it. I was secretly ashamed of my parents' accents, the way they were sometimes stared at in public, incomprehensibly, as though they were idiots or otherwise afflicted. Even though I looked the same as they did, with my narrow eyes and yellow skin, I knew that all I had to do was open my mouth and I'd establish absolutely that I was one of them—the gum-chewing waitress with her wide eyes and chapped lips, the cashier in the grocery store with the goatee and the acne-cratered scars across his cheeks. I wanted to dissociate myself as much as possible from my parents, from what I had come to see as their sad immigrant isolation, their outside-looking-in. I would not be the straight-A student, the geisha, or the coolie.

In school I studied the cool kids, the cheerleaders with their long hair and blank, bored faces, the football players with their hands stuck in the back pockets of their jeans. I observed the posture of idle prerogative: weight resting on the back foot, one hip stuck out, a hand held loosely at the waist. I copied as best I could their slow, minimal movements, as though an economy of energy were essential in staking an inalienable claim to birthright.

Double Box

When I was alone in the house, I snooped. In the night-stand by my father's side of the bed I found a *Playboy* magazine, a copy of *The Joy of Sex,* and *The Kama Sutra.* All were illustrated, and the images made me uneasy. I was dumbfounded by the women in *Playboy,* with their pink nipples and huge, globular breasts, and perplexed by the illustrations in *The Kama Sutra,* the pairing of monkey women and elephant men.

I tried to open my mother's red mother-of-pearl jewelry box, but it was locked. In the side drawer I found her birth-control pills—a foil clock with little white pills around the face. They were labeled with the days of the week; the empty slot with the last pill taken was six days before.

But these, treasures though they were, were not what I was after. I had a mission. I had already searched the downstairs, looking in the coat closet and the kitchen cabinets, in the Buddhist medicine chest in the living room, and behind the couch.

In the back of my father's closet, I found it. A square cardboard box sitting atop the highest shelf. I could reach it only by getting up on the chair in the corner and leaning over as far as I could, almost falling as I managed to ease the box down. I sat down on the floor and opened the box to reveal another box, white with white binding tape. Someone had sliced through with two crisscross lines so thin and straight they must have used a razor. I pulled the folds open revealing a nest of shredded paper; it felt strangely like opening a Christmas present. Underneath the paper, which I lifted out as carefully as I could, was a metal urn that looked like the bowl on my mother's bedside altar, only this bowl had a lid and, hard as I tried, I could not open it. I lifted the urn partway from the box and shook it. I felt the shifting weight of sand, heard the sound an hourglass makes, with a few clicks and pings, like small pebbles hitting the sides.

Stephen was in there. I tried to imagine his small body transformed into this metal container—not the container but its unseen contents—a few handfuls of beach sand and shell. My parents did not want him interred because they didn't know where they would end up. My father talked about taking the ashes to Korea, to the mountain where Sohns had been buried dating back generations, but my mother wanted him close, and so they had kept him, shoved away in my father's closet like a shoe box.

I put the box back and took it down sometimes when my parents went out. Depending on my mood, it made me glad that Stephen was still with me in some real way, or it made me so extravagantly sad that I would cry, the double box wobbling on my knees.

Last Try

My parents' hopes for a son, or for any more children at all, for that matter, ended the year after Stephen was killed. In the midst of what I now realize was a series of nervous breakdowns—or one extended breakdown in gradual escalation—my mother had an ectopic pregnancy, which resulted in her having her tubes tied.

I remember my father shaking me roughly by the shoulder in the middle of the night. He already had his coat on. I could feel the itch of wool on my neck. "Myung Hee-*ya*," he said, "your mother is ill. I'm taking her to emergency room. Mrs. Williamson will come in the morning to help you go to school. Myung Hee-*ya*, do you hear me?"

"Mmm-hmm," I said sleepily. My mother had been in

and out of the hospital so often that year that the news did not alarm me.

Later my mother explained. Instead of developing inside her uterus, the embryo had lodged in her Fallopian tube, which did not have the berth to accommodate it. She made it sound like a wayward child, wandering away from safety at the start.

I hardly saw my father the week my mother was in the hospital. Mrs. Park, Pastor Park's wife, came to stay with me, feeding me enormous bowls of *miyeok-guk,* seaweed soup, with rice and children's *kimchi.* She was a tiny woman with no hips or bosom, on thick, stocky legs, like tree trunks holding up a twig. Her English consisted of "please," "more," "wash," and "bed," lending themselves to combinations. "Wash, please," she would say, indicating with her hands in front of her face. "Bed, please," she would say, pointing at the clock. "More, please?" she would ask, with a paddle full of rice ready to dump on my plate.

When I finally got to see my mother, Mrs. Park took me to the hospital. She drove her husband's ivory Cadillac like it was a vehicle from God, forcing other cars to the side of the road as she sped fearlessly up their backsides. Her expression was neutral, even as drivers gave vent to their displeasure, and when we arrived at the hospital parking lot, she almost took out the mechanical gate before it had time to raise itself. I was indignant that my parents had allowed me to be so clearly endangered, and I lagged behind Mrs. Park going in the main entrance of the hospital, trying to make it obvious that I was no relation to this odd, haphazard woman.

At the doorway of my mother's room, Mrs. Park came to a

standstill and I was forced to stand beside her, looking in. My mother was lying in bed, her face turned away from the door. My father was leaning toward her, half on the bed, half off, his face close to hers, her hand clasped in his own. He was crying, or at least his cheeks were wet with tears, and this I had never seen before. Even when Stephen died, my father had put his face in his hands for a long time, but when he'd looked up, his eyes had been dry.

Now, his eyes gleaming, my father pressed himself closer to my mother, his head next to hers, resting for a moment on her pillow. They did not speak, and for several moments they did not move.

Mrs. Park finally cleared her throat and entered the room. *"Aegi-watseoyo,"* she said. *The child has arrived.*

Eyelids

When I was very young, my mother made me wear a clothespin at night to encourage my nose to form a salient bridge, instead of disappearing into the front of my face and emerging like a mushroom at the end of it.

"Please, God, give me a new nose, give me a new nose" was the nasal prayer I intoned, clothespin astride my face, feeling the futility and the force of my mother's optimism at one and the same time.

As my mother recovered from Stephen's death—the clothespin long since abandoned and my nose no less flat than before—she turned to new projects concerning my appearance. The chief objective was, of course, to render me beautiful.

My father made it clear what he thought of our efforts.

Once, when I was thirteen, he came in as my mother and I were discussing training bras. My chest was still as flat as Kansas, but I wanted to be ready just in case.

"I can make a bra for you, Myung Hee," my father said. "Two Dixie cups and a piece of string."

My mother gave him a withering look, but he persisted.

"How about peanut shells?"

"*Yeobo!*" my mother scolded, chasing him out of the room, trying to hide the smile that was edging the corners of her mouth.

Shopping with my mother was a type of sorority scavenger hunt. She had a genius for honing in on a bargain. She'd rifle through the racks at Macy's or Sears, pulling out garment after garment, which I would try on in the dressing room and trot out for her evaluation.

The clothes she chose for me were never things I would've picked for myself: black velveteen stretch pants with stirrups, a hot-pink-and-green-striped go-go dress with a pink vinyl belt, a gold paisley two-piece with bell-bottoms and a smocked baby-doll top. "Turn around," she'd say, doing a clockwise twirl with her finger. "Perfect," she'd pronounce, as I came back around to face her, nodding as though she'd achieved something monumental.

Though she seemed in most external ways to have recovered from my brother's death, there was something breathless about my mother's endeavors, a gleam in her eye that was close to a tear, a smile contorted into a look of agitation. She attached huge importance to insignificant things. Once when we were shopping, she pulled a skirt out of another woman's hands and refused to give it back. "I saw it first," she repeated, and bought it without even trying it on. Another time, when we lost one of our shopping bags, my mother insisted that we comb the mall for hours, retracing our steps and interrogating every salesclerk until, exhausted and embarrassed, I begged for mercy.

I began to pity my mother, and pity must mark an end to adulation. I saw her as smaller, reduced, no longer a goddess but a creature battered by tragedy. The story of her accident, the crucible of her destiny, took on new meaning. Instead of marking her for special fortune, it seemed a harbinger of a calamitous life.

On the second anniversary of Stephen's death, my mother spent all morning in her room. I worried when she did this because it often meant she was grieving; she would come out of the darkened bedroom with puffy eyes and pink nostrils, and when she spoke it would be with a slight stuffiness.

That afternoon, though, she emerged cheerful, her wigless head tied in a fabulous red chiffon scarf. She looked like a gypsy, with thick gold clip-on earrings and painted lips. She beckoned for me to sit beside her at the dresser and watch as she rimmed her eyes in black and smeared brown across the lids.

Unlike most Asians, my mother had eyelids; when she applied shadow, part of it would fold prettily inward. The effect was subtle but beguiling, a peekaboo of color in a crescent accent following the arc of her eyeline. My Mongolian fold was the bane of this effect. It was a stubbornly flat expanse of skin that hooded the eye, evolved to keep flying sand from blinding the Mongol horsemen, my impetuous, nomadic ancestors, but no good at all for the more sedentary art of feminine beautification.

My mother finished her eyes, squinting into the mirror with a satisfied assessment, and turned to me. Poised with the black kohl eyeliner in her hand, she looked into my face and sighed.

"*Aigo,* Isa," she said. "Eyes so small. You need operation like my friend Yeon Ja. Look much better. They make like this." She pinched the bottom of my eyelid and dragged it upward to demonstrate. "Just small procedure. Not a problem."

It was the first I'd heard her speak of this type of eye surgery, which many Asians were getting to give their faces that Western look. I stared at myself in the mirror, took both my eyelids and cinched them upward, trying to imagine what I would look like, what I would *be* like, if I gained that tiny indentation across the eye fold. I wondered if I would see more through these altered eyes, as though they were louvered blinds hoisted up to admit the view. I wondered if I would be beautiful.

That day my mother made up my eyes in extravagant Cleopatra black with long, sweeping curves at the outer edges, but when she painted across my hooded eyelids in "Fawn," the color just sat there in indiscreet patches, with none of the seductive shimmer and mirage of her own eyes.

"Isa," she said, and held up one index finger, as though I'd meant to leave. I watched as she reached across the dresser and unlocked the top of the red mother-of-pearl jewelry box she'd brought with her from Korea. Inside were little pouches of colorful striped satin that contained her most precious objects— brooches of green jade carved in fortuitous Chinese characters; an opal and sapphire ring set in eighteen-karat gold; a Mikimoto pearl necklace with a diamond clasp. She would take them out for me periodically, one by one, laying them lovingly across her wrist, or modeling them upon her hand, affording me an advance peek at my inheritance.

Now from deep inside this drawer, she took out a long envelope and counted out four crisp one-hundred-dollar bills. The multiple face of Benjamin Franklin, paunchy and good-humored, stared up at me from the fan they made among the bottles and jars on the tabletop.

"Don't tell your father," my mother said, pushing the money toward me. He was away in California, on the first of a series of collaborations with researchers at the University of California at Berkeley. "Save for operation now, Isa. This makes good start."

She patted my hand and smiled. "You'll be beautiful, Isa," she said. "You'll see."

So, as some kids saved up for cars or college educations, I began to save for eye surgery. Whenever I got money for baby-sitting, for birthdays or Christmas, I'd add it to the four Ben Franklins in the toe of a navy kneesock at the bottom of my underwear drawer. I'd look at myself in the mirror at night and imagine my eyes bigger, the veil drawn back, framed by expert shadings of purple, brown, blue, or silver, the world suddenly revealed to me with greater clarity and focus—as though by peeling back my eyelids I would gain genius sight, an amplification of vision like some superhero's power.

My mother would whisper to me about this transformation. It was a conversation behind my father's back, dreamy and perpetual. I sometimes had nightmares about the scalpel slipping, my eye slit in two like a boiled egg, and I'd be on the verge of telling my mother that I'd changed my mind; I didn't care that my eyes were small and creaseless, that I saw only the narrow view from beneath unadorned lids. But I never said anything. It seemed too important to her, some further dream of America she had fastened onto—an investment in the dream for the next generation—laying down roots to gain desperate purchase in pale, inhospitable soil.

Rachel's

I met Rachel in eleventh-grade science. We teamed up over Bunsen burners and pipettes, fudging the data and botching experiments, causing Mrs. Hendricks fits.

Rachel was brown-haired and hazel-eyed, with large breasts and a womanly figure. She lived with her mother and stepfather, two older stepsisters, a stepbrother, three ancient cats, and a Dalmatian puppy named Domino, in a house that looked like ground zero of the apocalypse but that I came to see as paradise.

The first time I went to her house, I was stopped in the foyer by her stepfather, Jerry. I knew he was some bigwig administrator at the Department of Higher Education, but he looked like a pot farmer. He was a thinner, older version of Jerry Garcia, with granny glasses, curly hair, graying beard, and the kindest face of any man I'd ever seen.

He was making bread in huge plastic bins. The first thing you saw when you entered the house was trash cans full of dough that strained over the rims, knocking the tops off. He was elbow-deep, kneading, throwing his whole body into it, as though he were rowing a boat.

"Hey, you must be Isa," he said in a booming voice that startled me. "Welcome!" He pulled an arm out of the muck and made to shake my hand. I hesitated. He threw back his head and laughed.

"Oh, come on," he said. "Get a little dirty! Give it a try. Here, stick your hands in. Punch and pull, like this."

I put my hands on the dough and gave it a few halfhearted pats.

"No, no, no!" Jerry objected. "You've got to get right down in there. Here." Beneath the dough I felt my hands being tugged under. "Like this," he said, manipulating my arms with his own. We moved for a moment together like pistons on a train; the dough was warm and yielding, and I was conscious of his hands attached to my own.

"That's better," he said, releasing me. He winked. "We'll make a baker of you yet."

Rachel's mother, Louise, ran a day-care center from an attached wing of the house, and there was a line of high chairs and a stack of plastic booster seats in the kitchen, along with counters of Gerber instant rice cereal, lunch boxes, rows of baby bottles with rubber nipples on paper towels, and plastic bags drying on the wooden spokes of a strange umbrella-like contraption by the sink.

At dinner everyone talked over everyone else, reaching across the table to help themselves to food, Domino going from place to place begging scraps.

"This is gross," said Gary, Rachel's nine-year-old stepbrother, sticking his fork upright in what appeared to be a bean-and-lentil casserole.

"Dad made it," said Adrienne.

"Which means it's extremely healthful," her father said, cutting himself a piece of one of his misshapen loaves of bread. "Lentils keep you regular," he said, and to emphasize his point, he farted.

"Dad, cut it out. You're disgusting!" said Audrey.

"This is a free-farting atmosphere, is it not?" Jerry demanded. He looked at me. "Isa, you're not uptight about passing a little gas, are you?" he asked.

I reddened and gave Rachel an anxious look.

"Isa's family doesn't behave like a pack of wild animals," Rachel said.

"Isa's family probably doesn't have grass and gravel for supper, either," Adrienne said.

"God, you stink!" said Gary to his father, waving his hand in front of his face.

"*I* don't stink. It's my farts that stink," he said.

Louise leaned toward me protectively. She was a small woman, but solidly built, with blond hair and red, pouting lips. She seemed to rise serenely above the chaos around her. "What's Korean cooking like, Isa?" she asked me. "I've never tried it."

"Remember the time when Dad confused the cat food for tuna fish?" Gary said. "That was *so* gross!"

Rachel rolled her eyes at me, and, though our plates were still half full, she got up. "Can we be excused?" she asked, and, without waiting for a reply, motioned for me to follow her downstairs.

The basement was one damp cement room outfitted with a stereo, black lights that made your teeth look purple, and a smelly green couch with most of its stuffing leaking out. Most important, it had a tiny black-and-white Zenith television with a rabbit-ear antenna.

I wasn't allowed to watch much television at home, so I was mesmerized by the flickering images that were almost always present at Rachel's. We were zealous devotees of *Dark Shadows,* the campy vampire soap that was on right after we came home from school. Barnabas Collins figured heavily in our fantasies, that dark, dashing figure of the undead. We watched *Gilligan's Island* and *The Brady Bunch, The Price Is Right* and *Let's Make a Deal.* We talked about Uncle Fester and Illya Kuryakin as though they were real people, and invented voice-over dialogue for the actors.

"Come here, you little crumpet, Alice," we had Mr. Brady say.

"I am wet with longing for you, Mr. Brady," she would respond, wielding a feather duster.

I was more intoxicated by TV than I was by the marijuana cigarettes that Rachel or her stepsisters, Audrey and Adrienne, would roll in the basement. The first time this happened we were watching *The Man from U.N.C.L.E.* while Rachel, who was a prolific artist, drew strange buxom women with outsized lower lips and voluptuous hair in different-colored felt-tip markers. I pretended not to be shocked as Adrienne lit up a joint and passed it to me.

"Aren't your parents home?" I asked, trying to sound like this didn't worry me so much as I was concerned on their behalf.

Adrienne, who was a sleepy-eyed brunette with the longest eyelashes I'd ever seen, shrugged, exhaling smoke through her nose. "Why should they care?" she said. "It's not theirs."

I took a tentative puff on the joint and tried to hold the smoke down in my lungs without coughing; it felt harsh and hot. I handed it to Rachel, who put down her pen and took a long hit.

Napoleon Solo was strapped to a conveyor belt, moving closer and closer to a rotating blade that would saw him in half from the testicles up.

"Isa's not used to this," Rachel said to Audrey, holding her breath to keep in the pot.

The Man from U.N.C.L.E.?

Rachel looked at me. "Freedom," she said, exhaling, and we both giggled.

What I remember most is laughing, laughing stupidly—from the pot and the freedom and the relief of being there—laughing until my stomach hurt and tears fell, with my head thrown back and my feet kicking in the air. We laughed until we had to pee, until some pee squeezed out and we cracked up about that, throwing pillows at each other and pretending to be grossed out.

I told Rachel and her stepsisters stories about my parents,

making them funny, skewing their peculiarities into easy carica-
ture, trading on their foreignness, their accents and their immigrant smells. "Remember, Myung Hee, don't stay out too late!
Study hard. Behave with dignity. You are Korean girl!" I would
mimic my father cruelly, exaggerating the *l*'s instead of *r*'s, leaving out articles, making him sound like some dim-witted
M*A*S*H extra. I betrayed the secret of my mother's wig. The
purple scar fascinated Rachel; she wanted me to give her its precise dimensions, a detailed description of its texture and shape.

Rachel started calling them "the Professor and the Diva."
We created their own television show. "Staaarrring Tae Mun Sohn
as the Professor," we would say. "And the lovely Hae Kyoung
Chung as the Diva!" We would roll all over ourselves laughing at
the inanities of the scenes we made up: my mother attacking
everyone she encountered with a makeup brush; my father fuss-
ily pushing numbers on a calculator. We staged mock versions of
Family Feud, with my Confucian forebears on one team and
Rachel's Puritan ancestors on the other. *"Which is worse, guilt or
shame? Survey says . . . !"*

Oh, it was terrible, what we did. My laughter was studded
with guilt, pricked with shame. I watched Rachel laugh and could
hate her for a moment, even as I laughed too, knowing that I was
pandering to her racism, that my betrayal cost her nothing, that
she was aware of no truth about my parents beyond what I told
her. It made the laughter more pungent, more bracing. It made
it necessary.

The first night I had dinner at Rachel's house was like a revela-
tion to me. I pretended to scorn her family, as she seemed to, but

I'd fallen in love with them all, especially Jerry with his salt-and-pepper beard and yeasty smell, his unseen hands clasping my wrists.

"My family doesn't even *have* bodily functions," I declared, making them all laugh. "I've never even heard my mother fart!"

"I want to come live at *your* house," Audrey said. "It sounds much more civilized."

"No, you don't," I said with sudden vehemence. "It's like they're embalmed or something! Like those sofas that people cover in vinyl so they won't get used."

Rachel and Audrey exchanged a look, and there was an awkward silence.

"Wow," Rachel said, after a time. "What a cool image!" She drew a picture of a couch with two people on it, a man and a woman, all of it encased in plastic wrapping, like cellophane. From beneath the covering, the couple looked out unsmiling, and underneath, Rachel scrawled, "Absence of Bodily Functions."

I took it home and taped it to my wall.

My Albino

At school they called him the Rabbit Boy. His real name was Herold Christopher Pettijean. But I called him Hero.

The most immediately striking thing about him was his albinism. He looked like Johnny Winter, with his long white hair and pale eyes. Because of his sensitivity to light, he almost always wore sunglasses, the aviator kind, which made him look even more like a rock star; in fact, he wanted to be one. He made a guitar in shop class, slightly boxy with a shortish neck. I heard him strumming it in a corner of the cafeteria. It sounded a little hollow, the sound reverberating inside like a penny in a dryer, but I found it impressive that he'd managed to make the thing.

He was exotic in an almost botanical way, like some rare orchid requiring careful monitoring of climate and temperature.

Teachers tended to fuss over him, students stared and made stupid remarks, but Hero didn't register any of it. He acted like he didn't realize there was anything different about him, as if it was the rest of us who were strange, with our inconsistencies of pigmentation, our unrestricted gazes.

Hero was almost six feet tall and whippet thin, with sinewy arms and large, strong-looking hands. He always wore black, a jean jacket, cowboy boots, and a black slouch hat that he wore indoors and that nobody ever told him to take off. He sat in the front of the room, where he could see the board, his long legs stretched into the aisle, translucent white wrists visible above where his hands were thrust into his pockets.

He whistled "Bell Bottom Blues" or "Lay, Lady, Lay" in the hallways between classes, and sometimes under his breath during exams. He was a virtuoso whistler. I would often linger at my locker just to listen to the end of a song.

Rachel and I mooned over him, though she acknowledged that he was mine. She already had a boyfriend—Dusty Jenkins, a varsity linebacker with a gold GTO.

"He's looking at you," Rachel would whisper in French class.

"How can you tell?" I'd say. "He has his sunglasses on."

"I can tell," she'd say. "He's looking over the tops. Ooo, *très formidable!*"

We would laugh, but my heart pounded so hard I feared it would come unmoored. In Hero's presence I felt my ordinariness, the awkward mortal geekishness that was beyond redemption, beyond cure. He was like a flash of quicksilver, a burst of sun too bright to look upon. He dazzled me.

I worked at the circulation desk in the school library during study halls. I was there one day, going through a stack of books that had just been returned. It was my job to find the cards on file and stick them into their back jacket pockets before they could be reshelved. I was also supposed to check out books for people. My hair was long and I wore it like a curtain in front of my face, peering out at the world from backstage.

Blume, Judy. Zindel, Paul. It was hard for me to resist reading the books I took from the wooden bin, pausing over the open pages and letting my eyes take in the words. It was an occupational hazard and one reason why the job appealed to me, that I could so easily lose myself in the middle of stories I might never finish.

"How do you see through all that hair?"

I looked up from my book and saw Hero standing there. It was something my father was always asking, and I felt a reflex indignation at the question, which I didn't associate with Hero's having asked it.

"How do you see with sunglasses on?"

He laughed. "I can't," he said. "But then, I can't anyway."

"You mean you're blind?" I said, stricken.

He smiled again and shook his head. He put his book up on the desk.

"Legally," he said, shrugging. "But I can see you."

I felt the heat come into my face, like a blast from a furnace, and I picked up his book to shield myself.

"*The Son of the Wolf,* by Jack London," I read. "He's good, isn't he?"

"My favorite," he said.

"I haven't read this." I took the card from the back of the

book and found the rubber stamp with the due date. I pushed it into the ink pad.

"You should," he said.

My hand was shaking as I stabbed the stamp onto the card, and when I took it away I could see that the date was blurred and ghostly. I stabbed the same way at the back of his book and pushed it toward him. He was looking at me from behind his sunglasses; I could see my face reflected in the dark mirrors of the lenses.

"My name's Herold," he said, leaving his book between us on the desk.

"I know," I said, and immediately blushed.

"And you are?"

"Isa," I said.

"Isa," he said, reaching for his book. "Thanks, Isa."

"Good-bye," I whispered. "Good-bye, Hero."

Breadmaking

Jerry and Louise became like adopted parents. I helped Louise with her after-school kids—taking them to the bathroom, feeding them graham crackers and juice. Rachel would be down in the basement with Dusty, and I'd be sitting on the orange rug in the day-care center, showing kids how to make origami frogs out of shiny colored paper.

I made bread with Jerry, kneading the dough like an expert, my arms submerged to the elbows in the trash cans. We broke off huge hunks, tucking them into oval loaves on aluminum sheets, and burning our mouths sampling straight from the oven.

"Why do you encourage him?" Rachel asked me. "I'm sick of his stupid bread. He's always sticking twigs and seeds and shit in it."

"It's not that bad," I said.

"Yes, it is. He's out of control!"

I didn't say anything. I couldn't admit how much I liked spending time with her stepfather.

"You know, Isa," he told me once, "the Papadakis men have been bakers for generations. They used to make this black bread that looked like bowler hats. You'd sink your teeth into a slice and they'd never come out again! You could play soccer with them."

His T-shirt was striped with sweat, his beard flecked with dough, the lenses of his glasses flour-dusted. "Isa, come here," he said. He crooked a finger. "You've got something right . . ." He leaned over to wipe my cheek.

"Hey!" I pulled away, laughing. He'd smeared dough across my face. I flung a glob at his beard, where it hung and fell.

"Why, you little . . ." he said, and patted my cheeks with two fully laden palms.

He would send me home with a loaf or two—pumpernickel or rye, anadama or caraway seed—but my parents preferred store-bought white bread for their breakfast toast and rice every night for dinner.

Casting Spells

I bought a book of spells for seventy-five cents in a used-book store and brought it to Rachel's for a sleepover. We were alone for the night—all the other kids scattered, Jerry and Louise at a party.

We made popcorn on the stove, with an excess of melted butter and salt, and looked at the book together. Rachel read over my shoulder, reaching for the pages with greasy fingers. It was impossible the amount of pleasure I got from the casual, sloppy grace of that house, the way the floors were always sticky and the air smelled of wet dog hair and bread dough, evidence of unruly life everywhere littering the kitchen counters, the rooms, the stairs, as though—like the popcorn and the bread dough—it must rise and pop and overflow its lid.

"Oh, definitely that one!" Rachel said, pointing.

"'Simple love charms to draw a lover to you,'" I read.

"For Hero," Rachel said. "*Your* Hero."

I felt my face go hot.

"Is there one in here for pushing a lover away?" I said. "You need that one for Dusty."

Rachel rolled her eyes. "Big horny bastard," she said fondly. She lowered her voice, even though there was no one else in the house. "He just wants to *fuck* all the time," she said.

"What?"

"Oh, Isa, don't be so naive!" Rachel said. "Me and Audrey went to Planned Parenthood. We're on the Pill."

"Why Dusty?" I asked, pressing the witchcraft book open with my palm. He was a dumb jock, and Rachel treated him with open condescension, complaining all the time about his stupidity and his preoccupation with football.

Rachel gave me a smirking smile and shrugged. "He just does it for me, that's all," she said.

We followed the instructions in the book, melting red candles and molding them into a ball. I murmured Hero's name three times and added a strand of my hair to the wax. All the time I was thinking about Rachel going all the way with Dusty, his mammoth bulk pressing down on her. What would it feel like, a penis pushing inside you? I thought about Hero's lanky body, his muscular arms and the delicate translucence of his skin, and I felt a rising heat, a queasiness in my stomach that was mixed with something else, something confusing, a dampness in my underpants.

I was envious of Rachel and somewhat in awe, not because

she was no longer a virgin, though that was part of it. No, it was more the notion that she could have sex and be so nonchalant, leaning over the table with one bra strap hanging off her shoulder, brown hair mussed and brushing at my neck. It was the assurance that I wondered at, the bold physical movement in the world, which I associated with Rachel's womanly body and her knowingness, her overspilling family and the chaos that seemed to me a statement of unyielding confidence and accustomed privilege.

I thought about my parents' careful house, the stillness and the silence as the three of us crept along the dusted furniture and the vacuumed carpets—as though we did not so much occupy the space as move within it like stealthy lodgers. If you left a glass on the kitchen counter for more than five seconds my mother would whisk it away, wiping up the wet ring on the Formica with a furious sweep of her sponge. Covering our tracks, removing evidence of ourselves. It seemed to me we apologized for our existence in the very way we lived, bowing and ducking as though to escape the notice of some vengeful god. It wasn't life that was lived there, but eternal penitence.

My fingers burned from the hot wax as I continued to mold it, catching the drippings as they fell onto the hardening ball, first the burn of pain and then a stiffening of wax on my fingers— a curious sensation but oddly sensual. I didn't really believe in the efficacy of the spell, but still I focused all my longing into that ball, shaping it in my mind's eye to contain every private hope, every stifled wish. I felt a catch in my breath as I thought of Hero's arms, a pull in the womb like the birth of desire.

. . .

Later that night, Rachel taught me how to masturbate with a pillow between my legs and two fingers pressed against me. She demonstrated beside me on the bed, naked beneath her T-shirt, the curls of her pubic hair spilling black to her thighs.

"Rub in little circles," she said, two vertical lines between her eyebrows marking her concentration. She made a soft moaning sound. "Yeah, that's right. Right there. Do you feel it?"

I was embarrassed. Cutie, the largest of the three cats, was lying on the floor across the room, looking at me with a knowing, slightly disgusted air.

"Doesn't it feel good?" she said.

I tried to ignore the cat and started rubbing through my underwear. I felt the warmth intensifying, radiating out from the circles my fingers described on my flesh. "Mmm," I said. It felt funny, like I suddenly had to go to the bathroom very badly; there was a tingling, a pulsing, and then a kind of pain that seemed unbearable. I let my hand stop. Rachel was moaning more rhythmically now, whispering to herself as her pillow jiggled up and down. I started again, until I felt a rippling sensation, and I shuddered at its passing.

Rachel, beside me, tossed and thrashed, entwined with her pillow, murmuring, "Oh, God, oh, God!" Her brown hair was everywhere, and I couldn't see her face. I was mortified but unable to stop watching her—where her hand disappeared into the pillow between her legs, where her back was arched and rocking. Finally, she screamed, a full-throated, desperate sound that made me sick with fear and excitement. She opened her eyes and smiled at me, brushing away her hair. Her face was sweaty and her eyes had a glassy expression.

"Did you do it?" she asked. "Did you get off?"

I nodded shyly.

"Isn't it great?" she said.

I could only blush, but I felt a quiet triumph. It would happen for me, the sweaty exertions and the grappling, the heat and the cooling of the flesh. Rachel wouldn't let me fall too far behind.

"Totally transcendental," I said.

Rachel looked at me for a moment, her face flushed and beautiful. "You crack me up, Isa," she said, throwing her pillow at me, and we fell into hysterics. Cutie, affronted, got up and left the room.

Transgressing

I started sneaking out at night, a tricky business given my father's insomnia and the hell to be paid if I was caught. I'd wait a couple hours after my parents had gone to bed, listening to the sounds of the house settling, of maple branches brushing the windows. I would listen until the quality of the silence changed and I could feel the whole house breathing in a sleep-charged monotone. Then I'd dress under the covers and creep downstairs, turn the handle of the door slowly, carefully, and slip out with my shoes in my hand.

At Rachel's, I would enter the garage and head directly down the stairs to the basement, where a group would already be gathered, listening to Donovan or Jimi Hendrix, getting drunk on Rolling Rock and cheap vodka. Sometimes we'd get high—

consuming bagfuls of chocolate-chip cookies and potato chips that Rachel's mom bought as snacks for day care—and watch late-night television, Johnny Carson and Japanese monster movies.

It was during one of these late nights that Hero showed up. Just the TV and the black lights were on and I didn't know who was coming down the stairs until I saw the purple of his smile, his hair underneath his hat, and the faint glow of his purple skin.

I didn't think he'd remember me, nor see me in the dark, so I said nothing until Rachel spoke up. "Herold, there's Isa Sohn in the beanbag chair. You two know each other, right?"

"From the library," Hero said, sitting next to me on the floor.

"Right," I said. "Jack London."

"Uh-oh, I think I forgot to return that book."

"That's okay," I said. "I'm off duty."

Later I was talking to Hero about the operation I was saving money for. "Asians don't have folds in their eyelids," I explained. "So they kind of stitch it up to make one."

"Why?" he said.

"So you can put eyeshadow on and it will sort of disappear," I said. "Like on Caucasian eyes."

He didn't say anything, but he didn't have his sunglasses on, and he was looking at me strangely.

"How much do you have saved so far?" he said.

"Almost eight hundred dollars."

"And how much does it cost?"

"A couple thousand, I guess," I said.

"I'll give you five not to go through with it," he said.

I laughed. "Why?"

He raised a finger and traced across one of my eyelids. "Because," he said, "I like your eyes the way they are."

I grimaced.

"Really."

"But," I objected, "you don't have five thousand to give me, do you?"

Hero laughed, showing purple teeth. "True, but I'd find other ways to pay."

I blushed. He said he liked my eyelids the way they were, without the added tuck, the winsome pleat that would open my eye and send the colored shadows back into the hollowed recesses of the lid. I believed him, and this sent a shiver of pleasure through me, that I could be liked for who I was and not for who I might be, for the reality and not some far-flung potential.

I told him I called him Hero and he was silent for a long time.

"I'm not," he said.

"I think you are," I said with such naked admiration that I immediately felt like an idiot.

"I've got oculocutaneous albinism," he said. "It's just something I was born with. It doesn't make me special."

I nodded, unconvinced, and he looked at me sharply. "I'm not just some curiosity for your collection," he said.

"Neither am I," I said.

He looked at me for a moment and we both laughed.

"Damn!" he said, and touched a purple palm to my cheek.

Hell to Pay

I lost my virginity at a Who concert, under a blanket on the lawn of the Saratoga Performing Arts Center. I told my parents I was going to a Fourth of July barbecue at Rachel's dad and stepmom's. Before I left, my mother gave me a shrewd look. I was wearing a sheer paisley-print blouse with low jeans and a jean jacket on top so my father wouldn't notice just how sheer or how low. I'd braided my hair and pulled it up away from my face, and put on some blush and lip gloss.

"You look like girl with secret," my mother said. "For Rachel's family you dress this way?"

I made a face. "I just want to look nice, Mom."

She continued to stare at me.

"There is a boy, Isa," she said. "I know." She patted my arm. "Go. Have a good time!" Her eyes were bright with complicity.

Driving up the highway, Dusty cranked the tape deck. "'People try to put us down, just because we get around . . .'" The windows were rolled down and Dusty was drumming his fingers on the roof of the car; Rachel had her bare feet propped on the dash. My hair whipped across my face, and my eyes stung from the force of the wind. I felt in love with the world, in love with my friends—Dusty with his dope-addled grin, Rachel, Audrey with her sweet, sad eyes, Hero in rock-star black with his arm around my shoulders.

"Let's just keep driving all the way to Canada!" I shouted.

"Yeah!" said Dusty.

"But we have to see the Who first," Audrey said.

"Who's on first?" Rachel said.

"'Talkin' 'bout my g-g-generation,'" sang Hero, using Rachel's headrest as a drum.

The parking lot was jammed by the time we got there, and people were pouring toward the gates. Lines were backed up as policemen went through coolers and backpacks. Like most of the others, we had no tickets. You could sit on the lawn for five dollars. I'd been to the ballet with my mother a few times, and there'd always been plenty of room between the islands of blankets and picnic baskets.

"Oh, God, look at this!" Rachel said. "We're never going to get in."

"Here," Hero said, handing me a blanket. "Me and Dusty'll go scout up ahead."

"Will you look at this!" Rachel said again. We were hemmed in on all sides. Scalpers called out, trying to get fifty dollars for seats; dealers, too, shouted, distributing loose joints despite the police presence a few hundred yards away; girls with painted faces danced in bikini tops and see-through skirts; people behind tables sold T-shirts and tapes.

I stepped up onto the base of a street lamp and scanned the crowd. It amazed me to see all these young people, their faces lit with maniacal joy, not looking as though they had escaped from anywhere or had to lie or answer to adult authority.

"Can you see them?" Audrey asked.

I jumped down from the lamp.

"Hey, Isa! Hey, Rach!"

Hero and Dusty ran toward us, waving their hands frantically. Hero took the blanket from me and Dusty grabbed the cooler. "This way," Hero said. He started scrabbling up a dirt bank. To our left we saw a place where the fence had been torn and trampled. People were streaming in. We followed Hero across.

"Hey!" came a booming voice behind us. "Come back here! You can't get in that way!"

We ran down the hill and onto the lawn, where there was not even a postage-stamp space between blankets. "Here," Dusty said, dropping our stuff on a piece of ground far from the stage.

We set out our blankets. Audrey went off in search of some friends who'd come up separately, and Dusty and Rachel decided to go explore. Hero and I said we'd stay and hold our spot. We got out some potato chips and a couple of Rolling Rocks. Hero lit his pipe and held it up to my lips as I inhaled.

"You're looking ravishing tonight, Isa," he said. He'd taken his sunglasses off, and his eyes were pink, naked-looking. I must've made a face, because he looked at me more closely.

"What's the matter, can't take a compliment?" he said.

I shrugged.

"Don't tell me no one's ever told you that before?"

I thought of all the times my mother had said it, *ippeo, ippeo,* like a mantra committed to memory, and yet for all that, I had never believed her. She was always talking about my eye surgery, and the way concealer could hide blemishes, and how a good haircut could make my face look slimmer. It seemed to me that beauty was a distant destination I might one day reach—with some surgery, plucked eyebrows, and a really great padded bra. And all the time there was the example of my mother, providing the evidence I needed of my own inadequacy, the tantalizing catalog of bypassed genetic combinations, of uninherited radiance.

I shook my head.

Hero looked scandalized. "Well, you better learn how to take 'em, girl," he said, "because you're going to be getting a lot more of 'em." He pushed me back onto the blankets.

Sometime during the night Rachel and the others reappeared. At one point I was dancing with Hero, an off-balance jumping-up-and-down dance with our hands pressed on each other's shoulders; another time we were looking toward the stage, which was filled with smoke and different-colored lights, and Hero was close in back of me with his arms around my waist.

The music was sloppy and raucous. "I Can't Explain," "The Seeker," and "I'm Free" from *Tommy.* We sang along reverentially, swaying on our feet like Weebles.

I was stoned, or drunk, or just high on the moment, but eventually I was lying underneath a blanket with Hero on top of me, my jeans and panties bunched down around my ankles. I felt the hard bone of Hero's hips, the smoothness of his belly pressing against me as his hands cupped my breasts beneath my blouse. His mouth slid across mine, tasting sweetly of pot, and there was such warmth and urgency to his kisses, a pounding of blood in my head and through my body, the music driving and pulsing, and the closeness of people in ecstatic communion, like a family of loved and familiar faces, rapt and approving, that I wasn't even shocked when I felt him push inside me, so hard and tender at the same time—reaching, straining, and not quite getting—to a place deep within me that I'd never fully considered before.

"Are you all right?" Hero whispered, after he'd shuddered and moaned and collapsed on top of me.

In truth it had hurt, but I didn't tell him this. I felt a stickiness on my legs that I thought might be blood. I looked around and saw blankets writhing and battling all across the lawn, great misshapen animals with multiple limbs trying to break free of tightly woven nets. I laughed.

"What?" Hero was laughing too, his breath tickling the back of my neck.

"Ert," I said.

"Ert?"

I giggled stupidly. "Opposite of inert," I said. "I feel very, very ert." I was afraid he'd laugh at me, but he just nodded.

"Like ruth," he said. "Instead of ruthless."

"Actually, I'm Isa, glad to meet you," I said.

"Glad to meet you," he said. "Isadora you."

We laughed, and kissed, and then grew silent. The music seemed to be coming from farther and farther away.

"What do you get when you cross an albino and a Korean?" Hero said.

"I hope we don't find out," I said.

"No, really."

"A Korino? An albean?"

He stroked my cheek. "Ertia," he said, "and ruth love."

Walking back toward the parking lot after the concert, Hero and I were entwined in a blanket. There was a thickness between my legs and I was conscious of walking bowlegged. I thought every-one must be able to tell what had happened to me. It was like I'd been relieved of some troublesome burden and initiated into a new society of Amazon women, with armored breasts and lethal thighs.

It took forever to get out of the parking lot. Dusty leaned on his horn and swore, and Audrey, who'd smoked too much pot and eaten too many potato chips, opened the door and puked outside the car twice, but Hero and I were in a bubble world where nothing existed except this besotted alliance we'd created.

We kissed the whole way back, and each time his tongue was in my mouth I felt a shiver, like an aftershock, between my legs, and I was thinking only about when next we might be able to meet, with nothing but our naked bodies and the hungry feel of his hands on me, the pushing in and the sliding out, like some wondrous new machine.

. . .

Dusty dropped me off on the corner of my street and I walked the distance to my house slowly. I knew I was in trouble when I saw the light on in the living room and the back of my father's head framed in the picture window. Even the angle of it looked angry, rigidly straight, propped there like a totem.

I fumbled with the key in the lock, and spent a long time taking off my shoes and hanging up my jacket in the hall closet.

"Myung Hee-*ya!*"

I climbed the five steps to the living room, where my father was sitting on the couch in his pajamas, his bare feet propped on the coffee table. He had a Korean magazine in his lap, which he let fall to the floor as soon as he saw me.

"Do you know what time it is?" His eyebrows formed a tight V in the middle of his forehead.

I shook my head.

"Where have you been?"

I stared at his feet, at his thick yellow toenails.

"Myung Hee-*ya!* Tell the truth!"

"I'm sorry I'm late, Dad," I said. "Mr. Shipley couldn't drive us home until all the guests left and—"

My father leapt out of his chair. He stopped in front of me, one fist raised.

"Your mother called your friend's house," he said. "The mother answered the phone. *Babo-jasiga!* She said you had gone out with some boys. She knew nothing about Fourth of July party!"

I heard my mother's voice calling from the top of the stairs. *"Yeobo, geureojima!"* Don't.

"You lied to us," my father said. "Where have you been?" His face was crimson and his hands trembled.

"I was at a concert," I mumbled. "I didn't tell you because I knew you wouldn't let me go."

"Stupid girl!" my father shouted. "Disobedient!" He flexed the fingers of his right hand.

I had the sweetness of Hero's breath on me still, and the vestiges of a high, and the thought that emboldened me was that this part of my life, the stifled, unhappy part that revolved around my parents and this house, was not the part that mattered any longer. Was not, in fact, a part of me at all.

"You never let me do anything, Dad. You think you're still in Korea, and you treat me like I'm eight years old! I'm almost an adult and this is America, in case you haven't noticed!"

"You're my daughter," my father said. He sounded out of breath. His words were deliberate, carefully chosen. "As long as you live in this house, you will do as I say."

"I don't want to live in your fucking house, then," I said.

"Isa!" My mother stood at the top of the stairs, clutching her bathrobe at the neck. I looked up at her and heard a crunch of bone to bone. My head snapped back to my neck and I saw yellow stars—it was just like in Sunday-morning cartoons when someone gets hit with a frying pan, yellow stars flickering and spinning, bursting behind my eyelids like firecrackers.

I staggered backward and fell to the floor. I felt a buzzing in my nose, and blood started gushing onto the pristine carpet.

"*Yeobo!*" My mother came running down the stairs and grabbed me by the shoulders. She started screaming at my father, all the while trying to maneuver my head back to stanch the flow. My father stood stunned in the middle of the room, fists clenched at his sides.

"What are you doing?" my mother yelled at him. "Are you trying to kill her? What is the matter with you?"

My father's face was the color of ashes. He looked shrunken, in his blue pajamas with the white piping, his chest concave. My mother screamed at him to get some paper towels and he meekly obeyed her, retreating to the kitchen and returning with the entire roll. She grabbed it from him, pulling off sheet after sheet to press against my nose, then got down on her hands and knees and started to daub the bloodstains from the carpet.

I was more stunned than hurt. My father's violence felt like victory to me somehow. *No matter what he does to me from now on,* I thought, *he can no longer reach me.* I felt myself floating far out beyond his command.

Sometime during my mother's ministrations, my father slipped out. We heard the garage door go up and the sound of the car whirring in reverse down our ill-fated driveway.

"You shouldn't talk to your father that way," my mother chided me gently. "He was worried about you."

She'd gotten a bucket of water and some rags and was working more seriously at the stains on the carpet. I was lying where I'd fallen, holding a mound of paper towel to my nose, swallowing thick, syrupy mouthfuls of blood.

I was looking up at the high ceiling, with its three wooden beams and the dark fan with cobwebs hanging from its blades. It occurred to me that it was the one place my mother could not get at to clean. The white painted surface was darkened in spots by soot from the fireplace, and there was a crack in the plaster that ran from the ceiling fan to the side of one beam, the ragged edges of which flaked and cracked like a raku glaze.

I'd lost a lot of blood and was feeling light-headed. Earlier that night I had lain on a blanket with Hero, looking up at stars. I could feel the dried blood stiff between my legs, and the dried blood on my face, sticking to the paper towel. Something about the crack in the ceiling seemed pitiful to me, hopeless, an irredeemable rift that penetrated deep through our house, and through our lives within it. I couldn't understand why we hadn't moved when Stephen died, why we hadn't fled this house with its visible fissure, its spreading wound.

"I'm sorry, Mom," I said, in a nasal, blood-thickened voice I did not recognize as my own. What I was apologizing for exactly I wasn't sure, but it seemed to encompass all I had done and all that I was to do, to cause her pain.

"*Gwaenchana,*" she said softly, brushing my forehead with a damp finger. *It's all right.*

I got up, washed my face, and went to bed. My mother gave me a hug in the doorway of my room. Sometime in the middle of the night I heard my father return, his footsteps chastened as they crept up the basement steps. When I finally fell asleep, I dreamed that the crack in our ceiling had widened and split, becoming a dark scar that traveled the length of the earth, a deep and ominous flaw reaching to the center of the world.

Candy Bar

The morning after my father hit me, I came down to find a Heath bar on the kitchen table.

"For you," my mother said. My father had already left for work.

I looked at it.

"It's his way of apologizing," she said.

"Well, whoop-di-do," I said, sitting down with my glass of orange juice and staring at the brown wrapper as though it were an encrypted message. *Eat this and all is forgiven.* I still felt the reckless mood of the previous night, the sense that I had passed irrevocably across a barrier that separated me from my former self.

My mother sat down across me with both hands wrapped around a mug of coffee. It was a mug I'd made for her in fourth grade, lumpy and blue-glazed with MOM in scratched-out letters.

"Your father has bad temper—" she said.

I rolled my eyes.

"But what you did was wrong, Isa," she continued. "You must always tell us where you are. Your father was so worried. We need to know you are safe."

"I was perfectly safe," I said curtly.

"You are our only child, Isa," she said, looking at me sadly. "So many bad things can happen. . . ."

The spirit of my dead brother, thus invoked, hovered between us like Exhibit A. It seemed to weight the air heavily, displacing oxygen. In my impatience, I envied his immunity.

"We only want to keep you safe," my mother said now. Her tone of voice was dreamy, her look unfocused, and I was filled with unaccountable fury. It was too much to take, this pocketful of stones she carried—the rounded stones of guilt and worry, the pointed stones of grief—the accumulated pile of which was more oppressive than the weight of my father's fists.

"You couldn't keep Stephen safe!" I shouted. "Even when he was right here at home, under your own nose. You couldn't keep him from being run over in your own driveway, could you?"

"Isa!" My mother's face blanched. Her hands shook as she held my mug to her chest. I felt winded, exhilarated and ashamed. I hadn't known myself capable of such cruelty.

Silence. My mother put the mug down on the table. She stood up. I noticed for the first time the fanlike lines in the corners of her eyes, the slackness of flesh.

I tried to keep hold of my anger, which had buoyed me with

a helium indignation, but already it was slipping. I felt sick. The awareness of the pain I'd caused my mother could not be repudiated; it seeped in despite my resistance, like noxious gas.

"I'm sorry," I murmured, but my mother only shook her head and left the room.

Self-improvement

My mother didn't speak to me for two weeks. She would enter any room I was in and look deliberately away, pursing her lips to leave no doubt that she meant to slight me. When I said something, she would sigh and shake her head, as though she couldn't quite hear. I tried to apologize in a number of ways: by cleaning my room, by not biting my nails, by offering, unbidden, to help with dinner. "Mom, I'm sorry," I said again after a few days. I was standing beside her while she stir-fried beef in a wok. "I didn't mean it."

She would not take her eyes from what she was doing, using wooden chopsticks like an eggbeater to turn the meat. Her posture was unforgiving. I waited her out. Finally she picked up the pan and shook the meat onto the platter with the vegetables and the noodles.

"Isa," she said, "call your father."

Around this time my mother started taking classes at Battrick Community College. She'd decided to finish her B.A. after all these years. Textbooks were piled on the kitchen counter, with different-colored spiral notebooks, mechanical pencils, and yellow highlighters. She pored over the academic catalog, circling courses titled "Literature of the Holocaust" and "Music Appreciation," soliciting my father's advice about "Science for Non-Scientists" or "Basic Chemistry." She even bought a BCC sweatshirt with the school logo embossed in orange.

My father was supportive of this new venture, favoring her getting out of the house and putting her energies into something constructive, though he wasn't happy about the prospect of her working outside the home.

"I could get a job as librarian," she said once. "Or doing research for professors. It would help with Isa's college."

My father put his hand out like a traffic cop. "Just take it one step at a time, Hae Kyoung," he said. "You don't want to tire yourself out."

One night I came down from my room to find my mother weeping in the living room, a copy of *Tess of the d'Urbervilles* on her lap.

"What's the matter?" I asked, wary of a rebuff. But my mother looked up at me eagerly.

"Oh, Isa, it's so sad," she said.

I nodded. In her BCC sweatshirt over her nightgown and white ankle socks cuffed with lace, she could have been a sorority girl. She turned her shining face to me, and her expression, despite the tears, was far from sad.

"So beautiful," she said.

From then on it was literature that possessed her. The same scene repeated itself, only the book would be *Les Miserables* or *Wuthering Heights, Anna Karenina* or *Pride and Prejudice.* Each time my mother would look up, lost and blinking upon my entrance, and announce the disposition of the characters to me as though they'd only just left the room.

"Mr. Darcy has just told Elizabeth he loves her," she'd say. "Cathy's married Edgar."

It made me uneasy, this new passion of my mother's; it had, after all, been my passion first. It was especially the quality of her passion, the precise ways in which it differed from my own, that made me balky. Whereas for me it was the language that transported: reading, a passion of the intellect, hovering above the page, my eyes on the words like an eagle's on prey—for my mother it was the purer passion of the dreamer passing through a dream, words banished altogether by the pulsing blood and the stirring of wind through scented trees.

Perhaps it was inevitable, given such a temperament, that my mother should soon turn from prose to poetry. I would come home to a recitation: "Because I could not stop for death . . ." or "I went out to the hazel wood . . ." She committed to memory the poems she loved best, stumbling over words and asking my help. "Is it 'Coole' like 'cool,' or like 'coolie'?" she'd ask me. "What does he mean by 'Echoing Greene'?"

She started to write poetry of her own, in bound notebooks that had BATTRICK COMMUNITY COLLEGE embossed in orange letters on the covers. She wrote so faintly, in mechanical pencil, that her words were hardly legible, as though she could barely stand to pin them down. "I stared at beauty in the wood/a reflection in a pool/and then one day it went away/and the wind blew cool" is a verse I remember, with the word "warm" crossed out before "wind" with three trembling horizontal lines.

She left the notebooks around the house, with a pencil clipped to the cover in readiness, and she sometimes read a poem to me out loud, with a shy kind of pride, and I would encourage her, or make some small suggestion. It seemed to me that my mother had a feel for lyric, though all her work had that quality—slightly generic images and subject matter—that suggested imitation. She grew particularly fond of Edna St. Vincent Millay, and wrote these lines on a three-by-five card that she wedged into the corner of her mirror: "My candle burns at both ends/It will not last the night/But ah, my foes, and oh, my friends/It gives a lovely light!"

One night after dinner, when my father and I were in the living room and my mother was downstairs finishing the dishes, my father suddenly grabbed one of my mother's notebooks and opened it with a mirthful expression. "*Yeobo!*" he called down to her. He held the notebook close to his face.

"Dad," I said. I reached for the notebook, but my father twisted away from me.

"'You whose lips I've kissed in summer/Think not that this is much/Such nectar from the flower/is what any bee may touch/Kisses in the snow/Mingled with the white of breath/These imprints linger longer/To keep until your death.'" My father read loudly, the intonation in all the wrong places, and when he'd finished, he gave a little laugh. "*Yeobo,* did you write this?"

My mother, who'd come quickly up the stairs, tried to take the notebook from him. Her face was flushed, and she wore rubber kitchen gloves that were dripping on the carpet. "*Yeobo,*" she said, "give it back."

My father ignored her. He skimmed a few pages and started to read again. "'The dancing women leapt and turned, and flickered on the wall/Their movements seemed to claim my soul and make me heed their call/I watched the light that streamed through space/the shadows falling late/And then a bang, a scream, a flame/and fire became my fate.'"

"*Yeobo!*" My mother grabbed at the notebook, but my father held her off.

"This isn't bad, Hae Kyoung," he said, one arm outstretched, reading to himself. He had a strange expression on his face, part mockery, part admiration.

My mother lunged and finally caught the notebook from him. "You don't know anything about it!" she said. Her hands trembled as she held the book to her chest. "Leave it alone!"

As she went back downstairs, my father tried to give me a conspiring look, but I returned a cold gaze.

Afternoons

Hero came to the house when my mother was in class. (I'd been grounded since the Who concert and wasn't allowed out.) I dug up my parents' copies of *The Joy of Sex* and *The Kama Sutra* to share with him. We giggled at the drawings of couples, impassive, naked, their bodies braided and supple. Finally we'd jump each other in my narrow twin bed, causing the headrest to rattle so violently against the wall that it left a stuttering of grayish scuff marks. We tried all the different positions, eager as Scouts to earn every merit badge—fellatio, cunnilingus, 69, standing up, kneeling, from the back, me on top, from the side, sitting in my desk chair, on the hardwood floor, even sodomy, which was not successful—I tore and he felt sorry, and I couldn't sit down for a week without pain.

I loved to watch him move his slim hips above me, his eyes closed in fervent concentration, the tip of his tongue poking from his mouth. His skin was the color of moonstone, with a subterranean sheen that seemed to make him glow. I imagined him inside me, his milky radiance chasing after the darkest corners, filling me with fulgent light.

We came to ourselves slowly afterward, dressing, straightening the bedsheets. He would whistle or sing silly songs like "Tie me kangaroo down, sport," or "I'm a lumberjack and I'm okay," while we remade the bed. My favorite was "I don't care if it rains or freezes / ' Long as I got my plastic Jesus / riding on the dashboard of my car . . ."

Hero was my plastic Jesus; his love made me feel invincible. We were opposites in many ways—he was Catholic, French Canadian, from a working-class family—but there was something deeply familiar about him to me. When I first met his parents (he called them "the Unit")—his mother a mousy brunette with a worn face and moist eyes, his father affable and large, a dark mustache and shaggy hair adding to his look of doglike devotion—I felt I recognized them. The way his mother fussed over him—"Wear a heavier coat, Herold, you'll catch a cold!" The way his father piled food onto his plate—"Come on, now, Herold, you're skin and bones."

We were different from those around us, treated like hothouse flowers. Our parents were overly solicitous, fearful, completely ignorant of what we needed—which was not necessarily one another, perhaps, but some approximate parole.

. . .

Hero was a reader, too, and a lover of language. I learned from him the words "oculocutaneous albinism," "Hermansky-Pudlak syndrome," "nystagmus," "esotropia," and "hypopigmentation." He taught me about the two Jacks—London and Kerouac—and forced me to stick with *Moby-Dick,* a book I found bizarre and ponderous, until I was finally caught by the mad beauty of it.

"Do you know what *Moby-Dick* is about?" he quizzed me after I'd finished it.

"Let me take a wild guess. Whales?"

He shook his head.

"Vengeance and undoing?" I said. "A guy with a grudge? Men on boats together way too long?"

"No." Hero smiled. "Nothing," he said. "The great void."

"You mean—"

"Nothing. That's it."

I thought I knew what he meant. All that expansive landscape, the obliterating whiteness of sea and sky, the ominous ever absence/presence of the whale.

"Well, if it's about nothing," I said, "it sure takes its time."

Hero laughed and began to sing. "'I can go a hundred miles an hour/Long as I got the Almighty Power/Stuck up there with my pair of fuzzy dice . . .'"

Flagrant

An afternoon in late March. Hero and I make love in my bed. We are off manuals now, having learned what each of us likes (Hero: kneeling in back of me with his hands on my hips; me: Hero going down on me, lapping in avid circles), with room for improvisation and fooling around. We act out our fantasies—the rock star and the groupie; Lolita and Humbert Humbert; the housewife and the meter man—starring in our own private porno movies, breaking the mood by laughing too hard.

Afterward, on this particular afternoon, we sit naked in bed while Hero rolls a chubby joint, swiping at its seam with his tongue. I get up to open the window. "It's snowing," I say. Hero gets up from the bed and hands me the lighted joint, which I inhale as he wraps his arms around me. We look out at the white that has settled on the lawn and across the black asphalt of the street. "It's so beautiful," I say.

"You are," he says, kissing the side of my neck. We sink back onto the bed.

Later we take a shower. I kneel to suck Hero's cock, gasping against the cascade of water. He pulls me up and runs the soap across my breasts and stomach. I can feel his hard-on against my ass. He enters me, lathery and wet; I have to stand on my tiptoes and hold on to the showerhead. When I come it's like being tossed, like waves breaking over my head and pushing me under. I am aware of Hero behind me, his orgasm whirlpooling around me; the voice of a sailor drowning at sea.

We towel each other dry. Hero reaches down to get behind my knees and ankles, between my legs. He kisses me there. "Your racing stripe," he calls my pubic hair. His fine, fair hair is slicked to his head, his pubic hair like a white beard dripping around his shriveled penis.

"We can call that one wet monkey position," I say, folding him up inside my towel.

"I got the banana," Hero says. He rubs his penis, already hardening, against my thigh. I laugh and throw the towel at him. The bathroom windows are painted with steam. I pull open the bathroom door and the vapor rushes to escape. I run for the bedroom, Hero right behind me, and there is my mother on the stairs, one hand clutched to the railing.

Jamming

Hero started a band called Choosy Mothers Choose Jif. Its members: Dusty on drums, leonine head, sullen, hulking. Adrienne on bass, picking her way through chords like she was negotiating a minefield. Hero on lead guitar, thin, dressed in black, with his pouting lips and dazzling Kabuki face. Audrey on lead vocals, fringed suede coat over miniskirt and cowboy boots, swaying with her eyes closed, her alto scratchy and sweet. I helped out with lyrics and attended all sessions, which were conducted in Rachel's basement.

> That strange flower, the sun,
> Is just what you say.

Have it your way.
Just what you say.

The world is ugly,
And the people are sad, baby.

That savage of fire,
That seed,
Have it your way.
Just what you say.

The world, it is ugly, babe,
And the people are sad,
And the people are sad, yeah.

It was our riff on Wallace Stevens. Hero rocked it out, singing backup to ethereal Audrey with his own crooning, Dylanesque whine.

"No, no, no, Aud." Hero stopped, and the other band members trailed off, Dusty crashing against the cymbals. "It's 'And the people are sad,' beat, BEAT. You're leaving out a beat."

Audrey chewed a hangnail. "Sounds better my way," she said.

Hero shook his head. "It messes up the rhythm," he said. "What do you guys think?" Dusty and Adrienne shrugged.

"Sorry, wasn't listening," Rachel said, doodling on her math homework.

Hero looked over at me. "What about you, Isa?" he said.

Audrey shifted her weight from one cowboy boot to the other. "Well, of course she's going to side with you; she's your girlfriend, for Chrissake!"

"Isa can be objective," Hero said. "She's got a mind of her own. What do you think, Isa?"

"I dunno," I said, distracted by European history. "What would Wallace Stevens think?"

Hero pulled his guitar strap from around his neck and put his guitar in its green velvet coffin, where it lay in state. "Okay," he said, "since no one else seems to care about the musical integrity of the piece, let's just call it a night."

Audrey smiled. "It's a night," she called it.

Canceled Class

My mother didn't say a word as Hero dressed and left. By this time the snow was coming down hard, the wind sending it in wild, roundabout routes, like feathers dumped before an oscillating fan.

"Classes were canceled," my mother said. She stood at the top of the stairs still, her book bag in her hand. Melted snow glistened in her hair.

"I have to get dressed," I said, surprised by the strength in my voice. I went into my room and put on my jeans and shirt. The bed looked incriminating, the sheets wrung and twisted; I retrieved the bedspread from the floor and threw it on top. Evidence of pot and sex was sweet and underlying despite the open window where the cold air strummed at the curtain. I lifted the window higher. Blood was pulsing in my head and my hands were shaking.

My mother didn't knock. She opened the door and stood there for a moment, taking in the bed, the smell, the window. Her calmness scared me. I couldn't read it. It didn't seem to mask anything, not anger, not shock. I wondered if she was doped on something.

"Isa," she said, "what is the matter with that boy?"

I had no idea what she meant at first. "Hero?" I said.

"So white, like ghost."

"He has oculocutaneous albinism," I said. I'd forgotten that she'd never seen Hero before; I'd forgotten what people first saw. "He's albino."

"Aiee, so white," she said. "Like dead person."

"Mom, cut it out. He's not dead and he's not a ghost. It's a skin condition, that's all. It's rare."

My mother shook her head. "That boy is unlucky, Isa," she said. *"Aigo, sireo!" I don't like him.*

"Mom, stop it," I said.

"No, you stop, Isa," she said.

I said nothing.

"Promise me you won't see him anymore."

"I can't promise," I said. "We're in love."

This seemed to rouse my mother. "If he comes to this house again, I will tell your father," she said, her voice rising. "And he will stop you from seeing him. Don't talk about 'in love,' Isa. You are too young."

"I'm not too young," I said. "Maybe you're too old, but I'm not too young!"

My mother put a hand in front of her face, as though to wave away an insect. She half turned as if to leave, but then she turned back to me. "What do you know about it?" she said, sounding a lot like my father. "Stupid girl. What do you know?"

Conspiring

Rachel got in trouble with Dusty. At a party for football players and their molls, she'd gotten drunk and made out with Danny O'Herlihy, the backup quarterback.

"Was he really mad?"

Rachel shrugged. "After he blew up at me, I think he felt better," she said. "I can't tell if he's more upset because I kissed another guy or because Danny's second-string."

"Is he going to break up with you?"

She gave me an exasperated look. "No way. Dumb fuck thinks he owns me."

"So, break up with him," I said. "That'd show him."

"The problem is," she said, chewing her lower lip, "I kind of think so, too."

· · ·

Hero and I sat in the library during seventh-period study hall, side by side at adjacent carrels, our hands working their way along each other's inner thigh. I could feel his erection against the corner of his jeans pocket. We propped books open in front of us in case Mrs. Johnson, the library aide, cruised by. Hero had his sunglasses on, and I stared straight ahead as though absorbed by the text in front of me.

Our not being allowed to see one another—my mother had actually employed Mrs. Williamson to come over in the afternoons when she was in class—had only heightened our passion, of course, and at least once a day a teacher tapped us on the shoulder and said, "PDA"—sometimes with a smile, like Mr. Felsenfeld, who wanted to show that he personally was cool with it but must reluctantly enforce school policy; sometimes with the swift redemption of a true avenger, like Miss Banyon, who had probably never had sex and resented the teenage hormones that loped, riotous and insolent, through the school halls. "PDA," she screeched, her talon fingers clawing at the point of contact, like one of the pod people in *Invasion of the Body Snatchers*.

Still we groped one another: by my locker; in the woods outside school, where we hung out before the final bell in the morning; at the south end of the library, where Mrs. Johnson, a fairly tolerant woman with teenage children of her own, patrolled the area.

I felt Hero's fingers edging up to the cross seam in my jeans, felt the wet heat gathering there, when he suddenly stopped, his left hand withdrawing to his own lap. He took my hand. "Isa," he said.

"Yeah?"

He took a breath. "My parents are talking about sending me to a school for the visually impaired. In Pennsylvania."

"In Pennsylvania?"

"I'd have to board there."

I stared. "But you're doing fine here, aren't you?" I said.

Hero shrugged. "They're bent out of shape because there's no real vision resource teacher here, and they tried to get one, but Mr. Gagne didn't keep his promise."

I glimpsed the future without Hero and felt something in my rib cage go hollow. "But you don't want to?" I said.

"'Course not." Hero squeezed my leg. "And I won't."

"So, what are you going to do?"

He gave me a sidelong look behind his glasses. "Leave," he said.

"What?"

"Come, too, Isa," he said. "Let's blow this joint. Make like Kerouac. There's a whole big world out there."

"You're kidding."

He shook his head. "My cousin Will's out in L.A. He's trying to get a band together. He says there're lots of jobs there for kids like us—lifeguarding, parking cars for rich people, stuff like that. You can make money waiting tables, and most of the time it's so warm you can sleep on the beach. I want to learn how to surf."

"You're crazy, Hero." I couldn't see his eyes, but I knew he was looking beyond the wall in front of him, to some sun-spangled utopia. "You'd get burnt to a crisp."

Hero smiled. "I'll wear sunscreen."

"Wow, you're really serious."

"Deadly," he said. "Name one thing to stay here for."

I thought of my mother and father and felt the downward pull of gravity. What I felt for them was too complicated to name, too difficult to provoke the simple word "stay." It seemed impossible to leave them. Perhaps it was necessary.

"Rachel," I said, thinking fleetingly of Louise and Jerry.

"She can come too," said Hero.

"But how—"

"Don't worry, Isa," he said. "I've got it all figured."

About a week before we planned to leave, my father scowled at me from across the dinner table. He set down his bowl of rice and placed his silver chopsticks parallel across the top.

"How are you doing in math these days?" he said.

"Okay," I murmured into my food.

"Any tests lately?"

I shook my head. Actually there had been one a week before on which I'd received an 84. The plan was to be gone before second-term grades came out, and I doubted I'd have much use for calculus in California.

"You don't bring home papers," my father said. "What kind of homework are you getting?"

"Yeobo," my mother said warningly.

"I just want to know how she's doing," my father said. "She needs to keep up grades for colleges."

"Isa's doing fine, *yeobo,*" she said. "I'm the one who needs help. This biology course, *aigo,* too difficult. What is this 'photosynthesis'?"

My father smiled indulgently. "I told you, Hae Kyoung, you should have taken physics instead."

My mother made a face. "All those atoms and invisible things," she said. "I thought plants would be easier. Something you can see and touch. Something real."

My father shook his head. "Physics is the foundation for all things," he said. "Nothing is more real."

My mother tossed her head. "What I really love," she said, "is my poetry class. That William Yeats. 'An Irish Airman Foretells His Death.' So beautiful!"

"Huh!" my father said, chewing hard on a piece of broccoli. "Poetry. What's real about that?"

"'Foresees,'" I said. "'Foresees His Death.'"

"Foresees," my mother repeated. "Foresees."

I thought about a week from now, where I would be. I tried to imagine what my parents would feel when they realized I was gone. Would the school call to tell them I was absent, or would they not figure it out until dinnertime? I thought they'd just give up on me, pronounce me wayward and ungrateful. It was my brother they cared about anyway, I reasoned. I thought of the double box on my father's closet shelf. Stephen's loss was the blow from which they could not recover.

Still, it was hard to imagine leaving them. The sound of my father clearing his throat in the mornings, the slap-slap of my mother's backless slippers down the stairs. I looked at them, at the way my father held his bowl to his mouth and shoved the rice in with rapid, economical movements of his wrist, the way my mother turned her spoon first away and then toward her before she brought the soup to her lips. The china pattern was white-and-blue floral; the spoons and chopsticks my mother had brought from Korea were silver with engraved flowers; the kitchen table was rectangular butcher block, scratched and white, with a split starting down the center seam. It all seemed more vivid to me, more real, now that I knew I would be leaving it. Even my father's baiting, his mulish challenge, was something I began to yearn for, to render nostalgic.

Rachel showed me a photograph she had cut from a magazine. Four women, in one-piece bathing suits and rubber caps with outsized rubber daisies attached, sat in the water playing cards. There was a table floating between them. The women were lying on their backs, their cards fanned out in their hands, in attitudes of total relaxation.

"That's us," Rachel said, pointing to the picture.

"Which one's me?" Hero said, peering over the top of his sunglasses.

"Do you know where this was taken?" Rachel asked.

"The Dead Sea?" I guessed.

"The Salt Lakes," she said. "I've always wanted to see them. You can float just like that."

"Is it 'Salt Lakes'?" I said. "I thought there was just one."

Hero nodded. "It's on the way," he said. "We can stop and see it."

I had never been west of Buffalo, so the thought of buoyant Utah lakes and crashing California surf was as theoretical to me as the moon landing. We were going to travel by Greyhound; Audrey would give us a ride to the bus station on Friday morning. The three of us, Rachel, Hero, and me, had pooled more than two thousand dollars, including the money I'd been saving for my eye operation.

Rachel seemed happy to be going. The trick was to keep Dusty at bay. She'd tried breaking up with him, but he refused to accept it. We laughed over the letter he'd written her. *I love you so much, baby, and I promise to give you a longer leash.*

"What am I, a dachshund?" Rachel had responded. She said it was just sex between them anyway. "Too bad it was so good," she said. "But it was never love, like you and Hero."

I felt my face flush, but in truth I didn't think there had ever been anything like me and Hero.

"Rachel?" I said.

"Yeah?"

"Do you worry about what's going to happen once we get there? To California, I mean?"

Rachel considered. "No," she said. "We'll be fine." She was silent for a moment. "We can always turn tricks if we get desperate."

I stared at her.

"That was a joke, Isa!" she said. "But I bet we'd do well. Once-in-a-lifetime chance to make it with an albino, a Korean, or a big-breasted WASP! Mix and match."

I laughed. "I think you'd get most of the business," I said.

Rachel shook her head. "Don't underestimate yourself, Isa," she said. "You're always underestimating yourself."

On the Road

I snuck a canvas duffel bag to Rachel's the night before we left. I'd been momentarily stymied by the prospect of packing for the rest of my life. What did one bring? What was essential for a life of bus travel and itinerant fruit picking, squatting in abandoned buildings and running from the law? Lots of underwear seemed crucial somehow, and socks, a few T-shirts, two pairs of jeans, a sweatshirt, a bathing suit in case we got jobs as lifeguards (though I was skeptical, as I had barely passed a YMCA swim class when I was nine).

A toothbrush, a tube of Crest, a hairbrush, and, for sentimental reasons, a powdered eye shadow kit my mother had bought me for my sixteenth birthday. "You can create eyelid with shadow," she told me. "Until your operation." I tried to avoid guilt by concentrating on details.

I packed a few books, and my journal, which I seldom wrote in but which I was now determined to fill with anecdotes and travel pieces to sell to *The New Yorker* and *National Geographic*. I had fondled words for so large a part of my life, I felt it was time to graduate to sentences.

My good-bye letter was brief and banal.

Dear Mom and Dad,

I'm with some friends and we're going to be fine. Please don't try to find us. It's nothing you did, so don't blame yourselves. It's just me, that's all. I hope someday we may meet again under better circumstances.

Your loving daughter,
Isa/Myung Hee

It struck me as I signed my double name that I was really two daughters, or—more accurately—half of one for each of my parents, and this made sense to me, adding to my conviction that my home life was irreparable, because I was only a half of something for each of them and could not become complete in the eyes of either.

I left the letter on top of my desk, propped on my stack of schoolbooks and my homework binder. I wrote on the envelope in big block letters—MOM AND DAD.

· · ·

Rachel wanted to bring all her art supplies, her Grumbacher pastels and spiral-bound sketch pads, watercolors, brushes, and wooden palettes.

"How're you going to lug all that across the country?" I asked. It was laid out on her bedroom floor like a display in an art supply store.

Rachel twisted the corners of her mouth and squinted down at the pile. She got out a mammoth suitcase, powder-blue plastic with shiny chrome clasps, and proceeded to put all her supplies into it. She closed it, picked it up by the handle and walked around the room. It was clear from the way she was leaning that it was heavy. She heaved the suitcase onto the bed, opened it up, and started pulling things out indiscriminately, then tossed in some underwear, socks, and a couple T-shirts.

"Okay, done," she said, and flopped down on the floor.

Hero brought a backpack and one small nylon gym bag. "It'll be warm once we get there," he said. "We won't need much." He kissed me, and Rachel made a face.

"Romeo and Juliet on the lam," she said. "And I'm the loyal sidekick, Barney."

"Oh, come on, Rach," Hero said. "We're the Three Musketeers."

"Right," she said, rolling her eyes. "Only I'm the one not getting any." She shook her head at us. "There better be some cute guys in California for me, or I'm going back to Dusty!"

"Are you kidding? There will be gorgeous guys everywhere," I said. "You'll forget all about Dusty."

"Dusty who?" Rachel said.

. . .

Audrey drove us to the bus station in Albany, hugged us good-bye, and waited on the platform while the driver put our stuff in the luggage compartment and we climbed into the bus. She was still standing there, waving, when the driver settled into his seat, adjusted his mirrors, and heaved the door closed. With a sigh of exhaust, the bus rumbled out of the station and into downtown traffic.

It was crowded on the bus and we had to sit near the back, Hero and me together and Rachel one seat in front. It smelled of pee and sweat, the kind of odors you associate with desperation and basic human need, and I felt my heart sink with the realization that this was what freedom might smell like, more like fear than euphoria.

A man in a green knit cap sat in a seat across and a couple rows back from us. He stared at Hero and frowned.

"Here we go," Hero said to me, squeezing my hand as the bus swung onto the interstate.

The man nudged the woman sitting next to him, a large woman in a red-flowered dress. He whispered to her and she looked at us, then whispered back.

"Some kind of hemophilia or something," she said. "They don't have any skin color, Tillis. Now leave him be."

But the man craned to see over me. Hero sat with his sun-glasses on and his hat pulled down low over his face. "Excuse me? Excuse me?" the man named Tillis called. I slumped down in my seat. Hero leaned forward.

"Sorry to bother you, man," Tillis said. He was smiling, but it wasn't a nice smile. His eyes were narrowed and his head, under the knit cap, was shaped like a bullet. "I've seen a lot of white people before, but I never seen a whiter person than you. Ain't that the truth? Heh, heh!"

I'd heard plenty of jokes at school about Hero. They asked him if his pubic hair was white (which, of course, it was), and sometimes they left celery or carrots in front of his locker, but mostly they were used to him by now, and his coolness and musicianship were respected. Outside of school, people were always staring at him, or looking startled when he walked toward them in a crowd, but they seldom said anything, and I never once saw him react. So I wasn't sure what he would do now, ten minutes into a daylong bus ride with Tillis on his case.

"Heh, heh, you're so white, you make most white folk look black," Tillis continued, more to the woman than to Hero.

"Shush, Tillis. You're going to hurt the boy's feelings," the woman said.

Hero smiled his slow smile. "That's okay, ma'am," he said. "Most people have never seen an albino before and they need to get a good look." Hero took off his sunglasses. "Go ahead, Tillis, knock yourself out."

"I apologize for my nephew," the woman in the red dress said. "He's a little . . . you know." She pointed discreetly to her temple.

"What? What you saying about me?" Tillis demanded.

"Nothing, Till," the woman replied. "Just that you're special, that's all."

Tillis looked suspiciously from his aunt to Hero. "Don't be calling me stupid," he said. "There's nothing wrong inside my head." He made the same gesture his aunt had made, but less discreetly.

"It's okay, really," Hero said, putting his sunglasses back on. He turned back toward the window.

I watched Hero in profile, staring out the bus window. I could see the pink of his eye, the delicate white of his lashes. I took his hand, but it felt lifeless.

It was not an auspicious beginning. Every time I had to go to the bathroom I saw Tillis giving me the evil eye. He stuck his feet out into the aisle to make it difficult to get by and muttered under his breath to his aunt, who didn't seem to be paying attention.

"China," I heard him say. "Chinese. Got a bunch of freaks on this bus, we do," he said. "Yellow and white. Got us a fried egg. Yes, sir, sunny-side up . . ."

I looked out the window, at the backward-vanishing landscape, the capitulating cornfields and pine forests, and I felt a queasy sense of losing something with each mile. I thought of that Simon and Garfunkel song, "Laughing on the bus, playing games with the faces . . . / They've all come to look for America . . ." Looking for America—what did that mean? I wondered. Where exactly did it reside? Had my parents found it, arriving not by Greyhound bus but by cargo ship and airplane? What was it I was looking for, or Tillis, or Hero?

I didn't want to admit I was scared. Scared to be away from home—nothing certain, nothing known—scared of being tested alone with Hero. It was strange that it had never occurred to me before, that the one thing I sought for myself, the thing I had craved from the time I noticed my difference, was anonymity, the blankness of an American face, an American recognition. And what had I done? Fallen in love with an albino. Whiter than white, brighter than bright, as foreign a face as my own, really, though in reciprocal quality. Together, instead of neutralizing one another—my melanin making up for his paucity—we were a comedy team, a punch line to a Darwinian joke, Tillis's fried egg sunny-side up.

We were somber on that bus. Rachel slept. Hero stared out the window long after the sun had set and the view dimmed. The sky filled with pigment, dark as Tillis and his aunt. Dark as, dark as . . . I tried to read, but the same paragraph seemed to repeat itself over and over—Brautigan's *Trout Fishing in America,* which I was reading for Hero, who claimed it was a great book. Something dark there, too, even with the hijinks and the humor. Looking for America. Looking at it. Looking toward it. Even as it eluded me, moving past, moving backward, nowhere to fix it, to find it, other than in my own mind's eye, the eye with or without the crease, the Orient, the oriented. . . . Looking but not finding. Finding but not keeping. Keeping but not possessing.

I woke up as we were pulling into a station somewhere in western New York. Hero nudged me and I waited until Tillis and his aunt got off before I reached across and woke Rachel, whose head had flopped sideways as she slept.

"I'm starved," Hero said. "Let's get some food!"

My neck and back were sore and I felt a jaggedness in my throat when I swallowed. Rachel groaned and opened her eyes wide to try to wake up. Only Hero seemed chipper. We got off the bus and bought a carton of milk and some Hostess apple pies, which we wolfed down in minutes. Hero kept the money, mostly in traveler's checks and twenty-dollar bills.

"I'm still hungry," Rachel said. "Let's get a burger."

"No time," Hero said. "Here, I bought a bag of pretzels and a thing of Gatorade."

"I hate Gatorade," Rachel said. "Tastes like piss."

Hero shrugged. "You can get something else," he said. He gave her a couple dollars.

Rachel salaamed and went off to the food counter.

"Hero," I said, "wouldn't it be easier if we each carried some money?"

Hero looked at me for a moment. "You don't trust me?" he said.

"Of course I trust you," I said. "It's just . . . Forget it."

"Because you can have it all." He reached into his pocket.

"Forget it," I said. "I don't want it. It's fine."

He stopped, his hand still deep in his pocket. "Okay," he said. "You know you can just ask me whenever you want anything." He put his arm around me and steered me back toward the bus.

Pennsylvania. Ohio. Indiana. Illinois. Iowa. Nebraska. The geography of the country became mostly internal for me. It was the ache of sleeping upright, the cramps in my legs, rough nap of seat fabric against my cheek, taste of unbrushed teeth, the chattering of strangers, and the continuous rattle of the bus engine vibrating beneath my feet. Outside, it grew lighter and darker, mountainous and flat, with fields and forests, farms and skyscrapers. But it was always outside, this landscape, mere backdrop for this metal capsule that shot through whatever scenery happened to be visible from the highway, traveling always forward, away from the land, away from the people, away from what seemed vital and tangible and real.

Intimacy

Rachel and I insisted on staying in motels, though Hero wanted to save our money. The rooms we rented were cheap and shabby, but at least we could take hot showers and sleep in beds and watch TV while eating take-out pizza. I half expected to see our faces on the local news, to hear that a dragnet of police was swooping down on the Buckeye Motor Court even as we stood washing our underwear in the sink. I imagined weeping interviews with our parents, my father monosyllabic with grief, Hero's mom wringing her hands. "We wanted to send him away to school," she'd say, "but we never expected him to take it this hard."

It was impossible to imagine that they weren't frantic with worry, and I tried not to picture the situation too closely from their perspective. *Please don't try to find us* was a pretty lame entreaty. As though they ever listened to me. And perhaps what I'd meant was the opposite. In a corner of my mind I felt this to be so, that I was making possible the means by which they might finally demonstrate, in some rousing, public fashion, that they really loved me. I imagined being reunited on *The Phil Donahue Show,* my father coming out from backstage with his arms wide open, tears streaming down his face.

Since my brother's death I had felt my identity to be "not-Stephen," a negative space, an absence, the living manifestation of my parents' loss. In an anonymous motel room in the Midwest, I was at least present, laughing and squabbling with my two best friends, who saw me as I wanted to be seen, as one of them.

We quarreled like siblings, especially Hero and Rachel, who were battling it out for Supreme Ruler of the Runaways. They fought about when to stop, what to spend money on, what bus route to take, what food to buy.

"I want ice cream," Rachel would say.

"We can't afford ice cream," Hero would reply.

"Of course we can afford ice cream," Rachel would say, enunciating slowly as though to a child. "It's only a buck."

Hero would shake his head. "It adds up," he'd say. "Besides, the bus is leaving."

Hero and I would stick Rachel's underwear in some guy's hamper at the laundromat, bury bogus love notes from Dusty in the bottom of her suitcase. *Rach—I love you and I promise I'll not only keep you on a long leash, but I'll feed you Alpo three times a day and take you on walks where you can pee on fire hydrants.*

Rachel would go up to people in bus stations—the biggest, most dangerous-looking guys around—and point to Hero. "My brother here says he can take you. I wouldn't try anything, though, because he's got this weird albino mojo." She would tell elaborate stories to people on buses about how we were outlaw Mormons and she and I were Hero's wives. We were on our way to Utah, she'd say, to join a community where polygamy was sanctioned and where there were four other women waiting to marry him. "It's wonderful," she'd say confidingly. "So much easier on us women!"

On a leg from Nebraska to Colorado, Rachel sat next to a blond cowboy skier from Aspen. His name was Nick and he had the windburn tan of an outdoorsman, with deep, craggy lines that made him look handsome in a squinting, Redford way.

"You should come to Aspen," he told Rachel. "It's fabulous. There are a million jobs working at the resorts. You could make a ton of money as a cocktail waitress in one of the bars. You'd be a hit!"

Rachel laughed. "What would I have to do to be a hit?" she asked.

"Honey," he said, "all you'd have to do is show up with a beer, wearing that smile!"

During a lull in their flirtation, Rachel came back to where I was sitting and whispered, "Isa, I really think we should go with this guy. He says there's all these jobs in Aspen, and everyone is, like, our age and we could find cheap places to share, and ski on our off-time—"

"You've only known the guy for five minutes, Rach," I said. "What if he's wrong?"

Rachel inclined her head toward where Hero was sitting. "What if *he* is?"

I considered. "Well, at least we've known him more than five minutes," I said.

I didn't hear them talking that much after that, but when I got up to go to the bathroom, I saw them making out, the cowboy's leather jacket pulled over their laps.

"Rachel's made a friend," I said to Hero, when I got back to my seat.

Hero shook his head. "He reminds me of that guy from *Midnight Cowboy.* You know, Jon Voigt? Not a lot upstairs."

"I don't think she's much interested in what's *upstairs,*" I said.

Hero frowned. "She's going to mess us up," he said.

"She's just lonely," I said, rubbing my hand on his knee.

"So you think we should just let her go off with Tex here?"

"No, of course not!" The thought had never occurred to me. "But she needs to have a little fun."

Deep into the journey, Rach came back. "I think I've persuaded Nick to come to California with us. He's psyched about maybe learning to surf."

"Absolutely not," Hero said. "He's not coming with us."

"Why not?" Rachel said. "You've got Isa. I want Nick. It's only fair."

"You don't even know this guy, Rachel. He could be an ax murderer."

"He's not an ax murderer," said Rachel.

"Okay, he's too stupid to be an ax murderer," Hero said. "But he's not coming with us."

"Then I'm getting off with him in Colorado."

"Oh, Rachel, don't do that," I said.

"Why not? Why do we have to do everything *he* says? Why can't Nick come with us?"

"Because he's a dumb cowboy you just met and you'll be sick of him the second you've fucked him; you know you will, Rachel, and then you'll be stuck."

Rachel stared at Hero for a moment. She couldn't deny that what he said was true, but she wasn't about to admit it. "Fuck you, Pettijean. Since when can you tell the future?"

"I'm an albino," said Hero. "We've got special powers."

In the bus station in Denver, Nick took his ski equipment off our bus—a long carrying case for his skis, a smaller one for his boots, and a large canvas bag of gear—as well as a small portion of Rachel's heart. They kissed good-bye like longtime lovers, she with her legs wrapped around his waist, he with his hands on her ass.

"You sure you aren't coming with me, darlin'?" he asked.

Rachel hesitated, glancing at us. She bit her lip and shook her head sadly.

"Well, I gave you my address, so look me up if you're ever passing through," he said, but I thought he looked relieved as he walked off.

There were tears in Rachel's eyes as she watched him get on

the bus to Aspen. "He was so gorgeous," she said. "God, those lips! And the way he talked. No one's ever called me 'darlin'' before!"

"Well, *darlin',*" Hero said, "I'm sure there will be many more cowboys as we head into the sunset."

"Yeah," Rachel said, mesmerized by the lingering sight of Nick's skis being hoisted out of the luggage compartment. "He sure was yummy. . . ." She shook herself out of it. "And I would have looked damn fine in one of those little cocktail waitress uniforms!"

"Tits for tips," Hero said, and made Rachel laugh.

When we stopped at a motel, two of us would sign in and the third would sneak into the room later. Sometimes we had rooms with two beds, but more often there would just be one—queen-sized if we were lucky—and we'd pile in. Hero was frustrated that we couldn't have sex with Rachel around. He would wait until he thought she was asleep and then creep his hand along my belly, down along the inner curve of my thigh. I would grab his hand and reroute it upward, and he would caress my breasts.

"We can't," I'd whisper.

"She's asleep," he would say.

"She'll wake up."

"We'll be vewy, vewy qwiet," he would say, using his Elmer Fudd voice.

"No, Hero," I'd say, pushing his hand away gently. "Shhh."

It was Rachel who brought it up one morning. "Hey, if you guys want to get it on," she said, "it's all right with me. I mean"— she shrugged—"somebody should be getting laid."

Hero shot me a look.

"Thanks, Rachel," I said, flushing, "but I think it would be kind of weird with you there."

"I could go out somewhere," she said. "I'll go to a coffee shop for an hour. Or is an hour enough?" She smiled slyly.

Hero nodded. "If you're sure you wouldn't mind," he said.

I shook my head. "Rachel shouldn't have to leave just so we can have sex," I said. "It's not right!"

They both stared at me. I couldn't help it—the idea of Rachel sitting in a coffee shop all by herself, watching the clock until the time she could come back to the room, depressed me. Rachel was my best friend and I didn't want her to feel excluded. I wanted to make love with Hero, too, and except for once with our hands under our jackets on the bus and one quickie while Rachel was in the shower, we had been largely celibate. Now that we were together, though, I felt patient. There was all the time in the world for that, I thought, in the brave new world toward which we were headed. I imagined encounters on the beach, Hero and I coupling in the warm ocean while the waves lapped against our naked bodies, afterward lying spent on wet rocks like basking seals.

"Let's just get there," I said now. "There's plenty of time. Rachel gave up Nick for us, Hero. We should be able to survive a few more days."

"No, really, I don't mind," Rachel said, looking from one to the other of us.

Hero shrugged. "If she doesn't want to, she doesn't want to," he said.

. . .

It was two nights later in a motel in Utah that I woke up from a vivid dream in which I'd been riding on a bus. Bright bluish moonlight came in through the curtains, and it took a moment to remember where I was. I don't think I entirely managed it, either, except to recognize that I was in another of a series of strange and inappropriate places far from home. It seemed we'd been gone for ages, but it had only been eight days.

I was settling back to sleep when I felt Hero's hand on me. I shuddered with the unexpected pleasure of it, his fingers brushing the surface of my skin with light, feathered strokes.

"Hero, no," I whispered, but he didn't stop. His fingers were dipping now inside me, first the fingertip, then the first joint, and the second, until three of his fingers slid in and back out, so slowly that I thought I would die from impatience. The sliding rhythm grew faster and rougher, until I felt the outward ripples that marked the edge of my orgasm.

I moaned quietly and grabbed Hero's hand from the back, twisting to face him. Only it wasn't Hero; it was Rachel. She smiled and kissed me on the mouth.

I closed my eyes, imagining it was a dream so I would not have to do anything to stop it. I felt Rachel's tongue against my breasts now, her hands having cleverly pulled the T-shirt over my head. The whole of my body was tipping to ecstasy like an overflowing of liquid. Rachel's lips and teeth surrounded my nipples, her fingers moved between my legs. I had to bite my tongue to keep from screaming.

I didn't dare open my eyes, but I knew now I wasn't dreaming. There were more hands on me, cupping my buttocks and caressing between my legs. I felt fingers joining fingers, stretching and slipping, pushing in counterrhythms. It was like being caressed by an octopus, all sucking tentacles, slippery, sliding, pulling me toward and against one side and the other. I felt no will, no distinct and separate self. I was part of this organism, this writhing, swimming thing, and there was nothing but texture and sensation and undulating fluid motion.

At some point I felt Hero's hands reach across my body toward Rachel. I felt a softness of flesh, a curve of breast, and I realized that my hands were on her, too. There was lovely thick hair along her legs and on the inner sides of her thighs. I remember thinking that she felt different from me down there, fleshier, more substantial.

Someone pushed me stomach-down onto the bed, and I shuddered as I felt Hero's penis press into me. It seemed larger than I remembered. He pushed hard, bouncing my pubic bone against the mattress, opening me up, thrusting deeper. I felt the labored sound of his breathing on my neck, rising in intensity, heightening my own excitement.

I heard a woman moaning and wondered if it was me, but it seemed far away, and my mouth was pressed against the pillow. I opened one eye and saw Hero's hand between Rachel's legs. I buried my head and screamed, the ripples pushing up to the surface now, bucking in waves of almost unbearable sensation—then there was the almost desperate letting go of Hero's climax, his belly tight up against my ass, the throbbing of his penis inside me, pulsing in spurts I could feel distinctly.

We fell asleep entwined, our juices stiffening the sheets,

bedcovers twisted and tossed, the shipwreck of the bed coming to rest on a tranquil sea.

The next morning as we were checking out of the motel, two Utah state troopers picked us up and took us to a juvenile detention center in a small town outside Salt Lake.

Locked Up

At the detention center, they went through our things. Anything sharp or potentially threatening was confiscated, including Rachel's skull ring, my ballpoint pen, and Hero's belt. We had smoked the last of our pot in Colorado the day before, and the worst things they found were a roach clip and a packet of Trojans. Hero was sent to the boys' ward, and Rachel and I were placed in separate but adjacent cells in the girls'.

No one wanted to tell us anything, not the bored woman who took our stuff, not the fat guard who locked and unlocked our cells. I called my mother and our conversation was terse. She said they were sending us plane tickets home the next day and we were to stay right there until they arrived. As if we had a choice.

My cell was cement-block gray, with room for a narrow cot and a toilet. Someone had written CARLY LOVES SAM inside a heart on the wall above my bed. How long it had been there was impossible to determine, and if Carly still loved Sam, ditto. I was scared, but honestly a little relieved to be delivered into the hands of the authorities. After what had happened the night before, I didn't know what things would have been like between Rachel, Hero, and me. Had the rules changed, or had it just been a onetime experience? I knew what we had done was not normal, was in fact considered by most of society to be sick and wrong, but I also knew that, in the moment, it had felt loving, warm, and generous. I didn't know how to face them, though, after that—my boyfriend and my best friend merging into one person. Every look, every word had to be reexamined in light of this new development. Was Rachel gay? Was I? Did Hero really want Rachel? Is that what all the tension had been about? It would make perfect sense to me—Rachel with her large breasts and straight fall of hair, her big eyes that were now brown, now green, speckled with yellow light. Against Hero's skin, my own body seemed sallow, a sickly color next to his pale, pearly translucence. Rachel and Hero were perfect together. They shared the same sulky confidence, moving boldly in the world, moving largely, as though striding across a doll's landscape.

That night I couldn't sleep. A million thoughts went through my head, oscillating between numb detachment and a terror close to clawing panic. I felt the walls of my cell collapse in on themselves, the air growing dense and fevered. I was sweating and shivering at the same time, rigid as a board on my narrow cot, as though by not moving, by not occupying much space, I could will myself to become calm.

Somewhere in the middle of the night, a girl in the cell across the hall started screaming and banging against the metal door. "Open the fucking door! I need my fucking cigarettes, you goddamn bastards! Open the fucking door! I need a smoke, you cunts, you sons of bitches! I got rights, you motherfuckers! Open the fucking door!" If her voice had been more melodic, she would have sounded like Janis Joplin.

I heard Rachel's voice from next door. "Give her a fucking cigarette and let us get to sleep!"

"Rachel?" I called.

There was a pause. "Yeah?"

"How're you doing?"

"—fucking cigarette—"

"Just ducky. You?"

"I'm fine."

"—motherfucking sons of bitches, give me my smokes—"

"You believe this girl?" Rachel said.

"I believe she wants her cigarettes."

"Why don't they just give them to her?"

"I guess they figure she might try to immolate herself," I said.

"Immolate?"

"Burn up, you know."

"Immolate," repeated Rachel. "You crack me up, Isa."

I spent the rest of the night staring at the ceiling, at a brownish stain that looked like it had once been wet, and a crack that ran its crooked length. The girl across the corridor screamed herself hoarse, hacking like the addict smoker she must have been, hurling herself at the door as though she would smash through it.

Looking up at the crack in the ceiling reminded me of the night my father had hit me and I lay on the floor waiting for the blood to stop. It seemed ages ago. The crack on our living-room ceiling had been straighter, finer than the one I was looking at now, and I remembered the sense I'd had of a tiny flaw, like a hairline fracture, sunk deep into the heart of the world. My father once told me that Korean potters purposely put a small crack or flaw in their pots to demonstrate their imperfection before God. It seemed to me an unnecessary gesture.

When I closed my eyes I continued to see the crack widening, overriding the light fixture, splintering the plaster, creeping along the walls and through the floor, burrowing down and down beneath the Utah municipal waterways and underground cables, wrapping around the girth of the world, surfacing for a moment on my living-room ceiling in upstate New York, before plunging to the dark earth's core. It would all split apart, I saw, along this narrow fissure, this tenuous line.

Sometime the next day they let us out, drove us in a squad car to the airport, and escorted us onto a plane. Our seats were not adjacent to one another for some reason, and we did not attempt to trade. Hero, behind his dark glasses, nodded to me as we got on. I nodded back and swallowed hard. *So this is how it's going to be,* I thought.

Rachel had been crying; her eyes were puffy and swollen and there was a red streak in the corner of one eye. She put up a hand as I walked by her seat, either in greeting or to ward me off. I couldn't tell.

When we got to Albany Airport, a police officer got on the plane to escort us off. I could see my parents and Hero's and Jerry by himself standing in the arrival area behind the glass.

"Guess my mom couldn't find anyone to sub," Rachel said, her voice cracking a little.

"This is *not* going to be fun," I said as we got closer. I could see my father's arms folded across his chest, his feet planted firmly apart.

Hero said nothing. He just loped toward the arrival area, his long legs carrying him far ahead of us.

Exit Hero

Back in school, we were celebrities. Underclassmen perched on tables in the cafeteria to hear our stories about the detention center: the girl rasping for cigarettes in profane language that Rachel would have to whisper in the hearing of the lunchroom monitors; a stain on the floor of Rachel's cell that she swore was blood; the manila envelope in which they stashed any possessions that could be deemed harmful.

"Why your rings?" one kid asked.

Rachel shrugged, looking down at her silver skull ring. "I guess you could swallow them and choke," she said. For in truth, it was mostly Rachel who held forth. I would sit beside her and confirm details, offering myself as witness should her veracity be challenged.

She liked to tell the story of Nick, the cowboy skier, with whom she had almost absconded to Colorado and a life of wedeling boyfriends and large tips. She embellished this particular story quite a bit, culminating in a marriage proposal in the back of the bus to Denver and a tearful (on Nick's part) farewell amid the thin blue air of the Rocky Mountains. I never said anything—what would be the point? There was something aggressive in the way she told the story that made it clear she felt she'd sacrificed something meaningful out of deepest loyalty to friendship.

Our parents forbade Hero, Rachel, and me from seeing one another outside of school. My mother cried. "How could you do this to us, Isa?" she said. "We didn't even know where you were!" But my father had been unpredictably calm. He'd hugged me at the airport, stiffly, but a real embrace, and later in the car he'd said, in a gruff, inconclusive voice, that he knew he was sometimes too hard on me.

"You're unhappy," he said, "you tell us, Myung Hee."

Audrey had stuck to our story about going south to Florida for as long as she could under the intense interrogation of all parents involved. She was just about to break, apparently, weighed down by guilt, her father's anger, and the anguish of missing Rachel, when the traveler's checks Hero used to pay for our bus tickets were found.

"That dumb shit," Rachel said when Audrey relayed this information to her. "I knew we should have taken care of the money. Traveler's checks! What a fucking idiot! His signature was like a fucking trail of bread crumbs."

I had noticed since our return that Rachel had adopted the speech patterns of the unseen girl in the cell across from ours, punctuating every few words with "fucking" or "asshole." I still loved Hero, though I was no longer certain of his feelings for me, and I could not blame him for doing what he thought was best just because it had turned out badly. And who was I to say it had? Personally, I was relieved to be home. I felt like something had changed in me. Perhaps I was suitably humbled by freedom, having glimpsed its vertiginous edge.

"It's over," I said. "You don't need to blame anyone. It's just the way it happened, that's all."

Rachel stared at me. She opened her mouth, then shut it. "I can't believe you, Isa," she said. "That asshole fucking raped me!"

Hero avoided me. He was never present during our cafeteria bull sessions, and in the classes we had together he would come in late and sit down without looking around. In any case, his dark glasses would have made it impossible to read his expression.

One day I touched his arm as we were leaving English. "Hero," I said, "can we talk?"

He pulled away as though I'd burned him.

We had been reading Edgar Allan Poe in class, and I suddenly felt sealed up, gasping for breath, like Fortunato in "The Cask of Amontillado." Poe captured the spirit of isolation I felt that day—which has, I believe, never fully left me. The pit and the pendulum, the House of Usher—a world of treachery, danger, and decay. The permeating smell of ash.

About two weeks later, Hero sought me out. I was in the library, the stuff for my senior research paper spread out all across the table. I was scribbling notes onto three-by-five cards—*Jean-Paul Marat, killed by Charlotte Corday in 1793. Had severe eczema, lung problems. Constant pain. Wrote in bathtub on wooden board. Received visitors in bath.*

I looked up because I felt a whoosh of air, and he was sitting across from me, dark glasses, as usual, blocking his eyes. I was startled by the delicacy of his features, the transparency of his skin, the shell of his ears, the painterly blue-white gloss of his hands.

I looked back down, continuing my notes. *Corday was tried and killed four days later. Executed by guillotine.*

"I'm going away," Hero said, so softly that at first I thought he'd said, I'm gay. "That school in Pittsburgh. I thought you should know."

My heart sank. It felt precisely like that. A fallen soufflé in the rib cage. An elevator dropping ten stories. I couldn't hide my shock.

"My God, Hero. When?"

He shrugged. "The Unit's shipping me off next week."

"Next week!"

"Yeah, they're 'finding it hard to deal with me.'" Hero gave the phrase a sardonic weight. Even behind his glasses, I knew he wasn't looking at me. He seemed to be staring at my note cards. *La guillotine—a more efficient method of mass execution, invented by French physician J. I. Guillotin just in time for the revolution.*

"They've always found you hard to deal with," I said, trying to spark a memory of prior intimacy.

Hero said nothing. He played with the end of a bookbinding, running his index fingers along its edge in opposite directions, then bringing them back together. I tried not to think about his fingers. Long, white, and deft.

"Yeah, well," he said. "I just thought you should know." He started to get up.

"Hero!"

He stopped.

"Hero, what happened?" I said. Without warning, tears. "I thought . . . I don't know what happened . . . I . . . ." I hiccuped the words between sobs.

He came around the table and leaned down to give me an awkward hug. He patted my back, and even in the midst of my distress, I noted the forbearance of the gesture, the attitude of vague detachment.

"It was a dumb idea," he said finally, straightening up. "What would we have done out there anyway?" He shrugged. "Don't cry, Isa. It just wasn't in the cards, that's all." He patted me on the shoulder one last time before turning to leave.

I sat there for a moment, the tears falling idiotically, though I no longer knew what for. I considered that he had not answered the question I'd been asking, and that he knew it, but what I judged him for most harshly was the terrible cliché he'd left me with— *"It just wasn't in the cards."* That of all the beautiful, funny, and tender things he'd said to me, these were the last words I would hear him speak.

Shadow Time

Without Rachel or Hero, I was set adrift amid the purgatory that was high school, without clique or definable group. I tried drama club for a while but found that I was not a particularly good actor, and that I in fact despised the overdramatic students who formed the core of the acting group. The girls seemed attracted to acting by vanity, the opportunity to strut and primp in front of a larger audience; the boys were drawn by ego, stroking nascent beards and arguing over motivation.

The artificiality of high school drama, combined with the woeful dearth of talent, made me feel like slitting my wrists with a dull butter knife. We butchered Chekhov; we annihilated Synge. Mr. Smallwood, the drama coach, had ambitions, but he couldn't turn a bunch of teenagers into anything like actors, and to be associated with such a lack of quality demoralized him, making him ill-tempered and weary.

I had a small part as the maid in *Washington Square,* and Mr. Smallwood became so agitated by one line he felt I was saying wrong that he actually tore up his script.

"No, no, no, no!" he yelled, tossing the rent script into the air, where it fluttered in pieces across the stage. "Good God, no!"

I tried the creative writing club, which put out the school's literary magazine, but dropped out after I got into an argument with one of the editors about a story she thought we should publish—a sentimental O. Henry–ish tale about a boy breaking up with his girlfriend, only to discover that she was dying of leukemia.

"It's terrible," I said. "It's badly written, it's melodramatic, it's completely unoriginal. It's mawkish!"

"Mawkish?" the editor said.

"I liked it," said another girl.

"Philistines," I muttered, and walked out.

A guy from my Euro class, Tommy Malden, asked me out. He was a soccer player, not handsome but pleasant-looking, with moppy brown hair and a slow smile. I couldn't figure him out, or why he wanted to date me, but I was grateful to walk down the halls hand in hand with him, and to make out with him at my locker before first bell.

I'd vowed never again to let myself be vulnerable after Hero, so I was surprised when after only a few torrid make-out sessions in the woods, Tommy reached over to stroke my cheek and said, "I love you, Isa." Etiquette required a reciprocal declaration, but

I knew, number one, that I didn't even remotely love him, and number two, that I'd promised myself never to use those words again. So I just smiled and kissed him.

My parents eventually let up their vigilance, sensing in me an apathy that they mistook for compliance. They even kind of approved of Tommy, who was sufficiently polite and deferential to pass as a good Confucian boy.

It was a shadow time, this period between coming back from Utah and the events leading to my parents' deaths. When I think of it I feel a cloudy numbness in my mind, a kind of partial amnesia.

Life, as they say, went on.

Unenhanced

I'd spent a lot of the money I had saved for eye surgery, so I was surprised when my mother brought up the subject again. I caught her staring at my face at breakfast one day, scrutinizing me as she used to, with a frank, appraising expression.

"Isa, I take you to surgeon," she said. "Dr. Cheon. He does eyes for many Korean women."

"I'm not sure I want to anymore," I said.

My mother shrugged. "No harm in appointment anyway. Talk to him. See what he has to say."

Perhaps I would have been less persuaded if it hadn't been for a casual remark Tommy had made a few weeks earlier. We had just finished having sex on the floor of his family room, and he was looking at me with that far-off look of sated desire, his head propped on an elbow above me. Sex with Tommy was somewhat of a letdown after my gymnastic performances with Hero, our virginity-ousting education in variety and excess. Tommy was a serious sort, considerate and tender in his own spartan way but not very imaginative in his sex technique. I tried to teach him a few things, but stopped when he pulled my head from his lap and, with a look of alarm on his face, said, "You don't have to swallow, Isa."

He liked straight-up missionary position, moving with the steady efficiency of a disciplined athlete. He had a nice, tight body, with finely developed calf muscles and a firm, square ass. Sex with him was pleasant, like a soothing bath; it generally had a soporific effect on us both.

We were lying quietly on the couch, the itch of the material impressing itself on my back, Tommy staring at me with a dopey expression. "What are you thinking?" I said, trying to sound more caring than accusatory.

He didn't answer right away, but caressed the side of my cheek with one finger. I expected some endearment, something appropriate to the moment, like how beautiful he thought I was, or how happy I made him—things he'd said before, awkwardly but in earnest. Instead he said, "Wow, your eyes are small. I mean, it's like your eyelids cover half your eyeball. How can you see?"

He spoke with a child's trusting candor, and I knew he hadn't meant to offend, but I was thrown into a rage. I sat up and started dressing, pulling on my socks as though I would go right through them.

"What's the matter, Isa?" Tommy said. "I-I'm sorry . . . I just meant, I mean, I think your eyes are beautiful, you know that . . . it's just . . ."

I buttoned my shirt crooked and didn't bother to fix it. "It's okay, Tommy," I said. "I know what you meant. I've gotta go, that's all."

I followed this with a week of the silent treatment. I didn't avoid him; I just wouldn't speak to him. He knew I was mad, but I wouldn't admit it.

I looked at myself in the mirror and saw the heavy-lidded eyes of a foreigner. *Slant-eye. Squint-eye. Chiney, Chiney.* I saw now that the reason I'd fallen in love with Hero was because he was a fellow freak, the only other person in school who could make me feel more ordinary. The bluish white of his skin, which I had once thought so lovely, called to mind a nest of maggots I'd once uncovered in a trash can, ghostly white and writhing. His pink eyes were often uncontrollable. They leapt and quivered and shook within their sockets, spastic organs sheathed in dark lenses.

I knew even as I thought these things that I did not believe them. I loved him still, and his beauty had been ethereal, almost sacred to me. I hadn't known why he'd wanted to be with me— that was the problem—and when he no longer wanted to, I could only wonder how it had lasted so long. I did not understand Tommy either, his quiet devotion. He'd meant no harm, I knew, with his remark about my eyes, but it had brought me back to childhood taunts, the teasing, my mother's patient explications of the Mongolian fold and its cosmetic pitfalls.

Eyes that looked out into the world, that took in so cleverly light, shape, and movement—why should it be important what they themselves looked like? The thing is that it was. Not what we see, but how we are seen.

Dr. Cheon was a walking advertisement for his business. The skin on his face was as taut as a drum; the folds of skin along his neck looked like they'd been pushed up behind his ears. I found the look a bit Dorian Gray, but it was remarkable how smooth and wrinkle-free his face was, like a mask of flesh more than flesh itself. He was also quite cheerful, smiling, I assumed, out of genuine good nature, and not because there, too, he had tucked and stitched an up-pointed curve of lip.

"Let's take a look," he said, holding my chin delicately between his thumb and forefinger. He turned my head this way and that. He nodded as he manipulated my eyelids, tracing a line horizontally from the bridge of my nose on each side, pulling them up to expose the hidden portion of my eyeballs.

"Very nice," he said. "I think we can do very easily." He paused and gave me a benevolent smile. "The procedure will not erase evidence of your ethnic heritage." He said this as though he had said it many times, and I wondered if he meant it as reassurance or caution.

"I will add an upper eyelid crease here and here," he said. A plastic head stood on his desk, with dotted lines drawn across its sightless painted eyes. He indicated with the fingertip of his smallest finger. "The incisions are tiny and any scarring is nearly invisible."

On the wall beside him were some before and after photos of women who had had the procedure. Dr. Cheon called it the "procedure," as though the fact that he was slitting your face open with a scalpel was incidental. The women's eyes stared out at me. They did look pretty good afterward, with a wide, direct gaze, eyelids pleated upward, their eyes larger-looking, more confident. Of course, he would put up pictures only of the successes. No botched jobs, women coming out looking like Cyclops, no wild, sightless horrors.

Dr. Cheon looked at me expectantly. His smile was beginning to unnerve me. "Shall we call your mother in now?" he asked.

Next to the photographs of women with before-eyes—hooded and sleepy-looking—and women with after-eyes—rounded with creased eyelids—hung framed diplomas. Johns Hopkins University and Columbia University medical schools. Board Certified American Board of Plastic Surgery, Board Certified Surgery of the Hand, American Society of Plastic and Reconstructive Surgeons, Inc., Lipoplasty Society of North America. "Sook Ki Cheon" in thick Gothic lettering across the creamy pages.

"Miss Sohn? Shall we call your mother in now?" Dr. Cheon repeated.

I looked at the plastic head with its androgynous features. Its eyes looked like it had been made up by a drunk, its staggered lines crisscrossing the lids. Dr. Cheon was smiling patiently, his face like stretched canvas; his eyes, as yet unenhanced, were veiled and did not seem as though they were smiling.

I shook my head. "Thank you, Dr. Cheon," I said, "but I've changed my mind. I don't want to go through with it after all."

Dr. Cheon looked confused. "But your mother—"

"She's not the one who'd be getting the *procedure*," I said. "I changed my mind. I'm sorry."

The smile returned to the doctor's face. "Well, certainly, if that's your decision," he said, ushering me to the door. "Good-bye."

My mother was leafing through an old issue of *Good House-keeping*. She looked up as I entered the waiting room. "How'd it go?" she asked. "I thought Cheon *euisa-seonsaengnim* said he would come get me."

"I'm not going through with it," I said.

"Isa, why not?" My mother looked crestfallen, as if I had suddenly declared I was dropping out of high school.

I shrugged. "I'm just not."

"But—"

"I'm not going to do it, Mom. I won't."

My mother smacked her magazine down on the table. The woman across from us looked up. "Waste of time," my mother muttered, as I followed her out.

That night I stared into the mirror above my dresser and looked at my eyes, first opening them wide and then squinting them to slits. I wondered what it would be like to look out at the world with Caucasian eyes. Would I catch things out of my peripheral vision, in the margins where my eyelids had formerly existed? If eyes were the window to the soul, as some poet had written, then what did it mean if you altered them? Would someone looking in be able to detect a different essence peering out?

On top of my dresser lay a few plastic rounds of colored eye shadows and some pencil-shaped eyeliners that my mother had given me, samples from cosmetics counters or shades she'd grown tired of. I had often practiced what my mother had taught me: how to create the illusion of an eyelid crease by putting a darker shade close to the eye and lighter shades underneath the brow. I had traced the outer curve of my lids with black kohl, smudging them slightly, looking, I always thought, like a baby raccoon. I gathered all these things into a heap now and swept them into the trash can.

Earlier that evening my mother had come into my room and sat down on the bed. "It's your decision, of course, Isa," she had said. "I just think you would look more attractive—"

"What's wrong with the way I look now?" I'd said, staring hard into the windows to her own soul.

My mother flushed and smiled. "Nothing," she said. "You are pretty girl, Isa. I just . . . It is always good to improve oneself."

What I had seen in her eyes disturbed me. She was lying. I realized that she was always lying. To me, to my father, to herself most of all. And it seemed to me at that moment that silence was the biggest lie.

"I'm not pretty, Mom," I said slowly. "You are, and I'm sorry if it disappoints you, but I don't want to change the way I look."

My mother seemed to consider this. She stared vacantly at a spot on the bed beside her, but she couldn't sustain it, couldn't take what I tried to offer. She got up from the bed and brushed the place where she'd been sitting, smoothing out the wrinkles.

"Of course you are pretty, Isa," she said. "Don't be ridiculous."

I broke up with Tommy. "I'm not interested in being in a relationship right now," I said to him. "I like you, but we don't have anything in common, and I don't think it's fair to keep pretending this is going anywhere."

Tommy seemed to consider this. As usual, I couldn't read his expression. He was quiet for a long time, looking somewhere in the vicinity of my chest. "It's all right," he said. "I was going to break up with you anyway. Don't take this wrong, Isa, but you're kind of spooky."

Poetic License

My mother was passionate about poetry, voracious about verse, rapt about rhyme. She came back from class flushed and fluttering, talking about William Carlos Williams, William Blake, and William Butler Yeats. Her poetry professor, Professor Moulten, was also a William, though my mother said he insisted his students call him Bill. This was such taboo for any former Korean schoolchild that my mother giggled when she tried it, and my father shook his head disapprovingly. "Professors cannot be too friendly," he said. "Lose respect."

"Professor—Bill—he wears blue jeans," my mother said. "For class."

My father frowned. "What kind of a professor is this?" he

said. He wore a suit and tie to class every day, with shiny black leather dress shoes.

"Oh, he's very good," she said. "And he's a poet, too. Look!" She showed us a dusty gray chapbook with a line drawing of a naked woman on the front. *Unspeakable Acts* was its title, brandished in slanted script across the top. "He wrote this book. He gave us each a copy."

My father made no move, so I took it. Inside, the poems were typed like on a normal typewriter. I flipped to one, "The Picnic." Its first lines: "My heart suspended in aspic / like your just dessert."

"Huh," I said.

"Today we discussed the famous poem by Robert Frost. You know it, Isa, 'Stopping by Woods on a Snowy Evening,'" she said. "We talked about how it is really about death."

I nodded. All I could think of was that Hero had once taught me to sing the words to the tango tune of "Hernando's Hideaway," from *The Pajama Game.* "Whose woods these are / I do not know . . ."

My father sniffed. "Poetry," he said. "No substance. Anybody can write a poem. It's just words."

"That's not true, *yeobo,*" my mother said.

"Well, it is if you don't care about the quality," I said.

"Quality?" my father scoffed. "Who can measure this quality?"

My mother sighed, took the chapbook back from me, and put it on top of her thick pile of books. *The Norton Introduction to Poetry. The Complete Poems of William Butler Yeats. The Poems of Emily Dickinson.*

"Your father doesn't like what he can't understand," she said to me, as though my father weren't in the room.

To my surprise my father smiled. "That's not true, *yeobo,*" he said, mimicking my mother's words of a moment ago. "I like *you,* and I don't understand you." There was something uncharacteristically tender in the way he said this. My mother lowered her eyes, pleased, and I felt as though I should leave the room.

Miscegenation

My father received a National Science Foundation grant for his UC-Berkeley project. I'd never been able to figure out what it was he actually did—something involving huge football field–sized machinery that cost billions of dollars, calibrating physical reactions to eighty-five decimal places. He tried explaining it to me a few times, but he would just start and my mind would recede into a cave, his voice echoing off the walls like the flapping of bats.

When the California team came to New York, my mother was required to host frequent dinner parties. There were various professors, graduate students, and post-docs, usually from places like Korea or Taiwan, who spoke little English and who were so appreciative of my mother's hospitality that they were literally dumbstruck.

My mother claimed to dread these occasions, complaining as she furiously cooked and cleaned that she wished my father would just take them to a restaurant. "So much less work," she would say, "and they don't know the difference!"

"Dad likes to show you off," I said. "He's proud of you."

My mother colored with pleasure. "Too much work," she insisted. "These post-docs especially," she said. "Eat like horses!"

Once they showed up, however, and my mother had changed from her apron and bathrobe into a simple black dress, she would radiate hospitality, basking in the attentions of the multi-aged men, juggling their needs, and coaxing even the shyest, most acne-scarred graduate student into a smile and a word of conversation. My father would beam from across the room with a tight-lipped expression of pride.

One night, during one of these functions, I found myself engaged in earnest conversation with a baby-faced post-doc from Korea. He had a broad, intense face, despite its smoothness and its youth, and eyes that burned with some inner vision. His hair was a little too long in front; he kept sweeping it out of his eyes only to have it slide down again a moment later.

"You like this writer, D. H. Lawrence?" he asked me, as I reached past him to refill my plate of *chapchae*.

It was such an out-of-context question, in such an out-of-place spot, that I didn't register what he'd said for a few seconds. He must have interpreted my lack of response as a result of his pronunciation, because he repeated, more carefully, "You have read this writer, D. H. Larr-rrence?"

"Oh!" I nodded. "Have you?"

"In Korean," he said apologetically, pushing his hair back. "Very difficult in English. I like *Women in Love.* Rupert Birkin. And *Sons and Lovers.* Very good."

"Have you read *Lady Chatterley's Lover?*" I asked.

"Oh, yes." He blushed.

I wasn't sure how to proceed from there, having run out of Lawrence books I remembered, but there was something so eager in the young man's face, so avid in his appreciation of this British novelist, that I felt I couldn't just take my *chapchae* and walk away.

"For a scientist, you're very well read," I said.

He smiled and nodded, but I wasn't sure he'd understood what I said. "My name is Lee Nam Ho," he said. "You are . . . Sohn Myung Hee?"

"Isa," I said. "My father's the only one who calls me that."

He gave me a quizzical look.

"I'm not sure why," I said. "My mother insisted on naming me Isadora—after Isadora Duncan, the modern dancer."

This time I was quite sure he was lost. He smiled vacantly and let his hair stay hanging in his eyes.

"You . . . ?" His thin face turned red. "You have boyfriend?"

I laughed. "No. Why?"

His face went from red to purple. "Dr. Sohn . . . um . . . your father . . ." he said.

"Yes?"

The young man seemed not to possess the English vocabulary to proceed. He swept his hair from his eyes and smiled at me, clearly embarrassed.

"You are beautiful," he finally managed.

"Mm-hmm," I said. I was beginning to understand. It was then I noticed that the young man with the baby face looked a bit like my father in the old photographs I'd seen of him as a young second lieutenant during the war. His hair was much longer, of course, and his face lacked the severity of my father's, but there was a resemblance I found unsettling.

"*Sillye-homnida,*" I said. *Excuse me.* "I have to go."

"I saw you talking with Mr. Lee last night," my father said casually the next day at dinner.

"Yeah, what exactly was that about?" I said.

My father shrugged. "You don't get to meet Korean boys," he said. "Mr. Lee is excellent student, from good family. He's a bright guy. You don't think he's handsome?"

"*Yeobo!*" my mother said in a cautionary tone.

"Dad, are you matchmaking?" I said.

My father frowned. "These American boys," he said. "That soccer player . . . You can have light fun with such boys, but in the end it is what you have in common that makes marriage last."

"*Yeobo, geureojima!*" my mother tried again. "Isa doesn't have to worry yet what makes marriage last."

"Dad, I'm only seventeen. I'm not planning on marrying anyone," I said. "And I have more in common with most American boys than I do with Korean guys who barely speak English."

My father put his hand up. "I did not say you should marry," he said. "But you need to start thinking about future, and heritage is important. A shared heritage. Maybe not someone like

Mr. Lee. I agree. He is from Korea, different culture will be a problem. But there are many Korean Americans like you."

"Dad, there isn't another Korean in my entire school!" I said. "If it matters to you so much suddenly that I marry a Korean, why don't we live in New York City or someplace?"

My father shook his head. "At the university, there are a few," he said. "What I'm saying . . ." He looked me in the eye, and I was startled by the obstinacy I read in his expression. "I would have difficulty accepting if you married Caucasian man. You're born here, but you are Korean."

"What about a black man?" I said.

My father smashed his fist down on the table. "This is not a joke, Myung Hee-*ya*," he said. "You think it's funny? If you marry someone I do not approve, you will no longer be my daughter!"

My mother started yelling at my father in Korean, her words so rushed I couldn't identify a single one. My father yelled back, their words overlapping, growing louder.

"*Michin-nyeon!*" I heard my father say. *Crazy bitch.*

My mother ran crying from the room, and my father followed after her. I sat at the kitchen table and listened to the sound of their voices, sharp at first, then gradually calm enough that I lost reception. What had that been about? Since when had my father started worrying about the purity of his ancestral line?

A little too late, I thought, thinking of Lee Nam Ho with his too-long bangs and flat features. He hadn't been bad-looking; he was actually sort of attractive in a gangling sort of way, but something inside me cringed at the notion of being paired with a Korean boy, his features matching my own like dominoes—the same narrow eyes, flat nose, and sallow complexion. I tried to imagine going to bed with him, our thin yellow bodies pressed together in perfect reciprocity, an incestuous twinning. I thought of Hero, of his strange pearl-like pallor, and I wanted to weep.

My mother apologized for my father's strange outburst the next morning. She was off to class, and my father had already left for the day. I had a sore throat and had decided not to go to school. "Your father thinks marrying a Korean will make your life easier," she said. "He means well, Isa. It's just his way."

"You always say that."

My mother sighed. "You think it's easy to live with your father?" she said. "He had difficult life—his father dying so young, then his mother and sister. . . . He gets angry, so angry sometimes because of these things he has lived. . . ." She didn't seem to be talking to me anymore. "Korean men are not taught to be tender," she said. "It's hard for them to show feelings on outside. That doesn't mean they aren't there."

"Sounds like a bunch of excuses to me," I said. "'Korean men aren't taught to be tender. . . .' 'They can't show their feelings. . . .' What you're saying is that he never has to change."

My mother looked at me and adjusted the strap on the book bag on her shoulder. She seemed tired. "I'm saying he never will," she said.

I had senioritis badly that spring. I wasn't excited about going to SUNY-Albany in the fall, but at least it was settled, and I would be getting away. We had an open campus at the high school, which meant that seniors could sign out during free periods. I would leave school at midday and walk home using the shortcut behind the Episcopal church.

Sometime after returning from Salt Lake I had developed a mild smoking habit. I would sit on a white birch stump in a small clearing off the path behind the church and light up, looking up at the sky and trying to train my eyes to find birds in the higher branches of the trees. Hero was remarkably good at this. He would locate birds by the sounds they made, mapping their location with alarming accuracy. "See that dead branch on the right of that pine? Just left and up, below that triangular space of sky," he would say, and like magic, I would suddenly see the bird resting there, as though he had conjured it with his words. I never understood how he did this, blind as he was to so much of the world, but he had unerring vision when it came to birds. He knew their names, too. Nuthatch and chickadee, purple martin and red-winged blackbird. Nothing very exotic. But I loved that he could name them. Like Adam in the Garden.

I tried not to think of Hero, but it was like not thinking about the elephant in the living room. He was huge in my mind still. That it had all turned bitter seemed only to have solidified him in my thoughts, to make me replay in my head the film reel of our love affair—all the passionate, exciting moments—and freeze it at the moment where it all went wrong, to see if this time I could analyze the precise thing I'd said or done, the mistake I'd made, the place where his heart had turned against me.

My father was in California again. The two research teams were going back and forth at regular intervals now. I imagined Lee Nam Ho awaiting my dad's arrival, contemplating D. H.

Lawrence's swooning passion even as his mind occupied itself with the fine mathematical calculations of the quantifiable world.

I started rereading *Women in Love,* which in truth I found a little too neat, a little too two-and-two. I'd read that Lawrence once said the problem with relations between the same gender is that there cannot be sex and the problem with relations between men and women is that there must be. At seventeen, I'd formulated the theory that it didn't matter whether you were male or female, having sex or not; the problem with relations between people was that the range of passion and disquiet was infinite in its variety, and none of us could escape the cell and the blessing of our own solitude. When I read Lawrence, I smelled a setup, ideas masquerading as characters, and I balked. Despite Lawrence's modern view of relationships and all that swooning, I thought it was, after all, right up Lee Nam Ho's alley.

One night when my mother was about to go off to an evening class, I asked her what she thought about love, and to my surprise, she blushed.

"Do you think it lasts?" I said. "I mean, with you and Dad . . . I know he's difficult, but he clearly loves you."

My mother closed her eyes. "Love changes," she said slowly. "Comes and goes. Not fixed, you know. Not like a mountain, more like ocean."

I nodded. "But after all these years, you and Dad still love each other, right?" My mother didn't answer right away. She was searching through her book bag looking for something. She brought up the chapbook I recognized from her poetry professor. She flipped through the pages until she found what she was looking for. "'Ask not of love,'" she quoted, "'for it will not answer.'"

I pondered this. My mother was smiling beatifically at me, as though she had not only trumped my question but taken all the tricks in the rubber. Did she mean, "Don't ask because I won't tell you"? or "Don't ask because the answer is no"? I held a dim view of her professor's poetry. I hadn't been asking *of* love, but *about* it, and it seemed to me that his syntax was off.

"I'm late," my mother said, glancing at the clock. She kissed me on the cheek. "Don't worry about love, Isa," she said. "It will find you."

It already had, but I didn't tell her that, and what I'd really been asking was, What do you do when it leaves?

She'd left her professor's chapbook on the counter, and I sat in the kitchen and read through *Unspeakable Acts* by William R. Moulten. I say I "read through," but really I skimmed it, or not so much skimmed as let my eyes land on a phrase or two. "Her hair falls / across the streambed of her eyes / like a shot horse; / the water grows bitter." These particular lines were underlined in black pen, as were the lines my mother had read out loud, "Ask not of love / for it will not answer." On the flyleaf, in a scrunched vertical hand, was written:

> To Hae Kyoung, who inhabits poetry like most people dwell in prose. All the way from Seoul, Korea, to Schenectady, New York—a propitious meeting and fond friendship.
>
> Yrs, Bill.

If I had been asked to write, as Dorothy Parker had been many times, a pithy review to sum up the contents of the professor's small book, it would have been this: "*Unspeakable Acts* is itself an unspeakable act, and certainly one which the reader wishes had also remained unwritten."

Was it my mother's simple lack of fluency that made her esteem his poetry so highly? It was possible. As a girl in Korea she was partial to sentimental poems that she was made to read in English class, poems by Edna St. Vincent Millay and Elizabeth Barrett Browning. But she was also the woman who claimed "Fern Hill" was her favorite poem, and she'd once asked me to read aloud to her "The Song of Wandering Aengus," and had been moved to tears.

Poetry, unlike science, was a subjective thing, I reasoned. One person's sublime was another person's ridiculous. In this my father was right. Who was I to criticize William R. Moulten? Still, there was something about him I didn't like. It wasn't just that I thought his poetry was bad, or that he revered Whitman, or that he taught at a community college; it was the inscription on the flyleaf of my mother's book. She'd said he had given a copy to each of his students. Had he also inscribed such personal notes on every one?

My mother's own poems were lovely, I thought, but now I wondered what they really meant. I'd helped her with one she'd written about *kimjang* in Korea, the season when the women make *kimchi* to store for the winter, the red peppers spread out on mats to dry on the roofs of the houses and in the dirt courtyards. It seemed vivid and evocative to me, though I had only seen the process in photographs. The last lines were "Salt and spice to heat the tongue/after a long winter's burial."

Espionage

Two nights before my father was due back from California, my mother didn't return from her evening class. I was worried because she usually got back by nine, nine thirty at the latest, and I thought she would call if she'd been detained. More like my parents than I liked to imagine, I was filled with visions of her car wrapped around a telephone pole, or some lurid murderer dragging her off into a deserted alley.

Earlier that evening my father had called, his telephone voice curt and efficient.

"Myung Hee, things all right there?"

"Fine."

"Is your mother home?"

"Tonight's her class."

"Oh, I forgot. Tell her I will be home Saturday night at nine thirty. Do you have a pencil?"

I got one. I wrote, *Saturday 9:30 p.m. Dad home.*

"Good. Don't forget to give her message."

Click. No "Good-bye," no "See you Saturday." Having reached the end of the information he wished to impart, he'd simply hung up.

I wondered if I should call him now. I had his hotel number in California. But what could he do so far away except worry? It was after eleven and I was already in my pajamas, having watched some terrible TV movie about a woman being terrorized by an ex-lover. It consisted of lots of long shots down dark corridors, the woman walking barefoot along the wooden floor, music thumping, the man lunging out from behind a houseplant to strangle her with piano wire.

I could call the police, I supposed, though it seemed a bit premature. There was always the possibility that class had gone over, that a few students had decided to continue discussion in some late-night coffee shop. She could have stopped at the A&P—open twenty-four hours—to pick up groceries. This seemed like my mother, that she would enjoy cruising the grocery aisles at eleven p.m., choosing carefully between Sanka and Maxwell House, in no hurry since my father was not waiting for her.

Even as I was thinking these things, I heard the garage door open and my mother's car, with its high idle, enter and then die. She came up the stairs from the basement with a light step (no groceries, then) and opened the door quietly, as though she expected I'd be asleep.

"Oh, Isa," she said.

"It's after eleven, Mom. Where've you been?" I said. "I was worried."

My mother put down her book bag and her purse and took off her jacket. She walked past me into the kitchen and started clearing dishes I'd left on the table.

"I'm sorry I'm late," she said in a bright, false voice. "Class went over and then Professor Moulten—Bill—asked some of us to come to his office to see his first-edition copy of *Leaves of Grass*." She ran a sponge under warm water and started to wipe the counters, her back to me. "Walt Whitman," she said.

"Mom, I know who wrote *Leaves of Grass*," I said.

"Yes, of course you do," she said. "I like it very much. 'Song of Myself.'"

"It's okay," I said, feeling contentious. "I mean, if you like folksy, self-indulgent windbags—"

My mother turned around. "He's Professor Moulten's favorite," she said.

"Yeah, well, I'm not sure Professor Moulten is that good a judge, to be honest," I said. "I read his book the other day. It's terrible."

It was as though I'd struck my mother in the face. Her cheeks actually reddened. She'd always trusted my opinions on literature, but here I was criticizing her guru, Professor Moulten—Bill. The unspeakable man. I felt a sudden desire to rip him to shreds before her eyes, to expose the sham of his poetic posturing and his great-man airs, his pompous self-importance so very at odds with the sparseness of his talents.

"Bill is very good poet," my mother said, slowly, carefully, as though she wanted me to memorize each word. "And he is great teacher."

I shrugged. "If you say so," I said. "Oh, by the way," I called over my shoulder. I'd turned away from her and was walking up the stairs to my room. "Dad called."

I lay in bed and listened to the routine patter of my mother's nighttime ritual, running water in the kitchen sink and washing the dishes (I did not feel at all guilty for having left them there), opening and closing the refrigerator door, her footsteps coming up the stairs, pausing outside my door but not entering. She went into the bathroom, and I heard the sounds of her ablutions, the soft motor of the Water Pik, the toilet's flush, water splashing in the sink.

It was a long time before I got to sleep.

My father returned from the West Coast without incident. The two of us, my mother and me, were solicitous toward him and watchful of one another. Together we asked questions about his California experiments, listening raptly to the answers, fetching his coffee and just-popped toast. My mother's poetry books, which had once spilled out along the kitchen counters, were suddenly removed. She began to talk most often of her biology class, which was difficult for her, and my father was delighted when she asked him for help.

None of this fooled me. I found a piece of Auden stuck into the zipped inner pocket of her purse, a line from Whitman folded into the back of her wallet. I snuck into her bedroom and found Moulten's chapbook stashed in the back of her bottom dresser drawer. The lines "Her hair falls across the streambed of her eyes / like a shot horse," were copied out across the inside cover, opposite Professor Moulten's inscription, in what appeared to be my mother's hand.

The next time my father went to California, I drove him to the airport. Dropping him off, I watched him grab his suitcases from the car. I pushed the trunk closed and we stood for a moment on the curb. My father's hair was thinning on top, a mottled swath of scalp beginning to widen along his part. It seemed too intimate a thing for a daughter to witness, and I turned away.

"Good-bye, Myung Hee," he said. "Don't drive too fast."

"I won't, Dad," I said.

The evening of my mother's next poetry class, I got into my father's car and drove to the Northway, got on and then off again, and ended up cruising by the unimpressive group of brick and concrete buildings that constituted the campus of Battrick Community College. I parked my car in the visitor's lot behind the admissions building. The buildings were conveniently marked with large white signs printed in orange letters, the signs more impressive and imposing than the buildings themselves.

It was a warm night, in the high seventies, and I strolled along, past the cement-block structure proudly marked LANGE LIBRARY, past the career services building that looked like a double-wide, past the sprawling brick hydra that was the Hutner Student Union. I tagged along at the end of a prospective student tour, listening to the backward-walking student guide describe the joys of foosball and air hockey, the convenience of the on-campus snack bar, and the thoughtful addition of a weight and exercise room.

I found the drab brick building that housed the English department at the edge of campus, at the point where BCC seemed to end and the town began. There was a pizza parlor across the street, and two doors down was a laundromat. At this point I knew what I was there for. I simply wanted to observe for myself, live and in the flesh, the esteemed Professor William R. Moulten, author of *Unspeakable Acts*. His chapbook did not include a photograph, nor any biographical information, and I was curious what this man looked like, how he moved in the world. I imagined some aging hippie with a William Kunstler hairstyle, in jeans and a handwoven shirt from Guatemala, sandals with white socks.

I walked into the building and found his name on the board in the front hall—WILLIAM R. MOULTEN RM. 24. There was a secretary in a glassed-in office on the left, but she didn't look up when I came in. I knew Moulten wouldn't be there because he was in class with my mother for another five minutes, so I mounted the narrow staircase, holding on to the handrail on the left. The stairs seemed warped and uneven, and my feet had trouble negotiating their crooked lie.

The door to his office was open, and no one else seemed to be around, so I popped in and took a look. It was a small room with a dormer window and a slanted ceiling, packed with books on shelves and in stacks on the floor. The metal desk was piled high with papers and books, and the only personal touches I could discern were a series of postcards of black-and-white portraits thumbtacked along the side of a bookcase. One I recognized as Dylan Thomas, curiously wrapped around some sort of sticklike tree, looking like a particularly woeful Saint Sebastian. Another I knew was T. S. Eliot, with his owl eyes and banker's uniform. Walt Whitman was there, of course, with his madman's hair and beard, containing multitudes.

I heard voices and footsteps coming up the stairs, so I quickly slid out of Moulten's office and around the hall, which doglegged to the right, and, standing outside Sally Baldwin's office, pretended to be searching for my paper in a pile on a chair marked WILDERNESS LIT.

"Of course, it's not quite so straightforward, Helen," I heard a man's voice say. It was a deep voice with a trace of a Southern accent, and it sounded so pompous I had to believe it was Moulten's.

To my surprise, I heard my mother's answering giggle. "It never is, Bill," she said. "I've learned that much."

Helen? I'd never heard my mother called that. Hae Kyoung. I suppose it was close enough. But it made me cringe. *Helen.* As though he couldn't pronounce her real name. As though he had decided to rechristen her; the poet with the power of naming. Helen, after Helen of Troy, destroyer of men and cities.

"The thing about Stevens . . ." I heard him say, and the door closed.

I waited for five minutes, ten, fifteen. I wore no watch, so I had no way of knowing exactly how long I waited there, standing frozen with Lisa Flanagan's paper, "Thoreau's Views of Nature in *Walden*" in my hand.

Finally I crept back down the stairs. The door to Moulten's office was solid wood, its public face barren except for a color cartoon from *Doonesbury* that I did not take the time to read.

I left the English building and went across the street to sit in the pizza parlor, at a table by the window. I ordered a slice and a Coke and kept careful vigil as I ripped the pizza to shreds with a plastic fork and swirled the ice in my cup. The incurious proprietor wiped tables around me, looking up at frequent intervals at a ball game blinking from a television anchored in the wall.

Several people went in and out. At one point I saw the secretary leave the building and walk slowly down the street to the parking lot. I had no idea what time it was at this point, but I believed my mother and her professor to have been in his office for easily two hours by now.

I was just about to give up and go home, my stonelike anger having given way to a kind of disgust at myself, at them, at the whole sordid stakeout I had poisoned myself with, when I saw them leave the building together, my mother and her professor. Helen and Bill. He was a tall man with hair the color and texture of an ocean sponge—not at all what I'd expected. From where I sat I couldn't tell how old he was, though he seemed younger and squarer than I'd imagined, in a plain white shirt and chinos, with ordinary brown shoes that looked like Hush Puppies.

They stood outside for a few moments, laughing about something, and then they began to walk, slowly, in the same direction the secretary had earlier. At the corner of the street they stopped. He leaned forward and kissed my mother, briefly but unmistakably, on the lips, and my mother put her hand up to his cheek. Then he crossed the street and kept walking, and my mother entered the parking lot, found her car, got in, and drove away.

Accusation

I raced home from BCC at eighty miles an hour to make sure I was back before my mother, who was a notoriously slow driver. I didn't know what I would say to her, how I could admit I knew what I did without forfeiting a large portion of the moral high ground. I felt such a tremendous rage, it was like a tumor blooming inside my heart. Even so, I wasn't sure why. Was it that my mother was cheating on my father? That she was infatuated with a bad poet? What was the source of this gruesome passion that shook me, bodily, like a hurricane force, so that even as I drove down the highway, I had to hunch over the steering wheel with both arms, hugging it for ballast?

. . .

My mother got in a few minutes behind me, bright-eyed and breathless. "Oh, Isa, hi," she said, closing the door to the basement behind her. She stepped out of her shoes, put on her slippers, and hurried upstairs to put away her books.

I followed her into her bedroom. She'd taken her wig off and was placing it on its Styrofoam head. She scratched at her scalp, in back where her scar was, and began to brush her real hair, which was dulling to gray beneath the black. She looked up at me. I was standing in the doorway.

"Isa, what is it?"

"I saw you," I said.

My mother gave me an uncomprehending look.

"I went to Battrick. I got back just before you did. I saw you with him."

My mother sat down on the bed, the brush in her fist still poised toward her head. She said nothing.

"I saw him kiss you," I went on. "I heard him call you Helen. He was talking to you like you were a second grader, something about Wallace Stevens." Something compelled me to keep speaking, as though to prove to her I had been there, that I'd compiled hard evidence against her. Still she said nothing. She began to brush her hair again, slowly, looking not at me but toward the sliding closet doors.

"He's a lousy poet," I said. "That book of his is the most pathetic bunch of crap I've ever read. No wonder he teaches at a community college, so people like you will look up to him and treat him like this great man, when he knows he couldn't write a good poem if his life depended on it. I bet he preys on women like you every semester, picks out the most adoring in the group, gives her his book, tells her what great stuff she writes—"

My mother raised the hand with the brush. "*Josim-hae,*" she said in a low voice that did not sound at all like her. *Be careful.*

The pitch of our breathing heightened. I was aware of the white of my mother's knuckles as she gripped the hairbrush above her head, the red flange of her nostrils. Her eyes flickered and then narrowed.

"Go ahead," I said, my voice steady.

My mother said nothing, but brought her hand down, and I walked out of the room.

Note

I drove back to Battrick. This time I parked in the lot beside the laundromat, next door to the English building. The doors were locked and the place was dark. I went across the street to the pizza parlor and borrowed a pen and a blank paper place mat from the fat proprietor. There were more customers now, college kids in booths watching the game on television, chattering among themselves, pouring pitchers of beer and hoisting pizza slices from the soggy rounds of cardboard in the middle of their tables.

The pen the man had given me didn't work at first, its ballpoint stopping and starting like a bad transmission. I had to scribble along the top to get the ink to flow.

Professor Moulten (*I wrote*):

I know all about your affair with your student "Helen" Hae Kyoung Sohn. If it does not end immediately, I will be forced to take the matter to the Dean and to Helen's husband, Dr. Tae Mun Sohn, who has a black belt in tae kwon do and no reverence whatsoever for poetry.

A concerned party

I folded the note several times and wrote WILLIAM MOULTEN across the blank part. I walked back over to the English department and hesitated. I wondered if the secretary was the kind of person who would unfold and read a note addressed to a professor before putting it neatly in his box. Or maybe one of the other members of the faculty would come in early in the morning. Would they pick it up? They probably all knew already. It was a small college; it was probably the gossip of the campus.

"Look who Moulten's doing now. That pretty Oriental in his poetry class."

"God, he didn't give her a copy of his chapbook, did he?"

"Of course. He always does."

My face burned at the indignity of it, the public humiliation. I felt it on behalf of my father, and my mother, and on my own behalf, the single living child of their failing union. I stood there, poised to slip the note under the front door of the office, where it would lie in the foyer until someone bent to pick it up. I wished I'd thought to bring an envelope, but all the stores were closed by now, and it occurred to me that Bill Moulten, being the kind of person I knew him to be, would probably find a note like this amusing. I couldn't stomach the thought of becoming a joke at his expense. In the end, I crumpled the note and threw it in the trash can on the corner of the street where I'd seen a strange man kiss my mother.

Ultimatum

My mother came into my room the night I returned from BCC for the second time, having failed to deliver a note to her lover. She knocked and I unlocked the door. She was standing in her robe, holding a piece of dental floss in both hands.

"Isa," she said, "don't do this. I will give him up. It's wrong, I know. I just needed . . ." She started to cry. She sat down on my bed and bowed her head; she wasn't wearing her wig, and a sober vein of gray opened at her part. I felt the thrill of my righteousness, but I felt pity for her also. I thought of the months of grief after Stephen died. The way she had looked then was the way she looked now, like misery itself feeding from its own subterranean source.

"Are you in love with him?" I said. "You can't be in love with him! I mean, God, Mom."

"You don't understand, Isa," my mother said quietly.

"Obviously not."

She patted the bed next to her for me to sit down. I remained standing. "You remember you asked me," she said, "if love lasts? And I said it changed."

I glared at her.

"I love your father. He is difficult man; you know that, Myung Hee-*ya*. He does not show his feelings, he has bad temper sometimes, but he is a good man and he loves me, I know." My mother stopped, readjusted her position on the bed by shifting her hips slightly. "People change, Myung Hee," she said. "You will learn. Marriage is a hard thing, because what you want when you are young is maybe not what you need when you are older."

I considered this. It was strange that she was calling me Myung Hee.

"So what do you need now that you aren't getting?" I said derisively.

My mother blushed and looked down at her lap. "You know, Myung Hee, before the war came, I was young girl, and I had been in this bad fire, and everyone said no one would marry me. And there was this boy, the brother of a friend of mine, and he would watch me when I was walking to school, and one day my friend gave me a note he had written. He wanted to know me, he said. He thought I was pretty. I did not write him back. But the next time I saw him I smiled, and when I went to my friend's house we talked and once we held hands for a few moments, and I thought he was the most splendid boy I had ever seen."

"And?" I said.

"He was killed by Communists," she said. "In the first days of the war. He was a poet, too sensitive to fight."

"A poet?"

My mother smiled. "I know what you think, Isa. Yes, he wrote poems, but that's not what I mean. He was a poet by his nature. He could not survive war." She looked down at the piece of dental floss in her hand. "I think sometimes that he was my great love," she said. "By the time I met your father, I did not think so much about those things."

"So you never loved Dad?"

My mother made a face, her expression equivocal, unconvinced. "I loved him," she conceded. "Only it was different feeling. With your father I felt safe. He was so sure, and he loved me so much. And he was very hurt, your father, underneath his pride. I think I knew . . . I knew about your father, that there were things we didn't understand about each other and that he would not try to understand, and that was good for me."

"What about Bill?" I said.

My mother pulled the dental floss taut between her fingers. She spoke slowly, deliberately. "You say Bill is bad poet," she said. "I don't know. I cannot judge. But he talks poetry to me. He tells me I am beautiful. He makes me feel beautiful." She closed her eyes for a moment. "One day you will know what this means."

Of course I felt I knew what it meant already, and this rekindled my anger. I thought of Hero and tried to banish the feel of his hands on my body, the light that radiated from his skin. I banished also the fleeting image of my mother lying under William Moulten, his white hands engulfing the brown swell of her breasts. I thought of my mother's fascination with those dancing caryatids, despite the fact that they had ruptured into flame and almost taken her life. I thought of the way, the morning I'd had the premonition of my brother's death, I had accidentally smooshed a moth against the back of my hand, how its pale body had rubbed across my skin, adding an unlikely sheen, an opalescent light. I shook my head.

"Look," I said now, "you *are* beautiful. You know that. Dad certainly thinks you are. The thing is, what you're doing is wrong. What if Dad found out? Don't you realize what you're doing?"

My mother looked at me with a level gaze. "He won't find out," she said.

"How do you know that?"

"Because I am careful. And because he is busy with work."

"What if I told him?" I said.

"You won't," she said.

"Why wouldn't I?" I said.

My mother smiled. "Because we are women, Isa, and we know how to keep secrets."

"It's not my secret!" I shouted. "They're never my secrets! 'Don't tell your Dad,' whenever you buy a dress or a new pair of shoes. 'Don't tell your Dad,' when you dent the car. 'Don't tell your Dad,' about the money you have stashed in your jewelry box! I'm tired of keeping all your fucking secrets!"

"Isa!" My mother looked at me in shock, but it was as though I could see her only from a great distance, and instead of feeling pity or sympathy or love, or any of the emotions you'd think I might feel—the daughter who had looked to her mother all her life with adoration—I felt only disgust. She started to cry then, harder, her tears turning to sobs, a great keening grief, and I saw the flaw that extended throughout the world open upon her face.

Graduation Dress

A few days before my father came back from California, my mother took me shopping for a graduation dress. She was, as usual, quite insistent about what she felt would be most flattering on me—something white, she thought, tea length, with a flared skirt and some lace on the sleeves. I kept mumbling that I was going to be wearing a long robe on top anyway, so what did it matter what I wore underneath?

"Oh, Isa," my mother said with a trace of her old cajoling, "every girl wants beautiful dress for her graduation day!"

"Not every girl," I said. "Not me."

My mother looked at me. She started to say something but stopped. She hugged the few dresses she'd chosen to her waist as she zipped through another rack, her fingers flying as though across an abacus.

I loitered in the large, fluorescent-lit space, glancing at price tags, running my fingers across fabrics. I watched other women, with my mother's same frantic pace, hoisting garments over their shoulders in a fireman's carry.

We had spoken no more about William Moulten since the night of my discovery, and I wasn't sure whether my mother had broken it off yet or not, but she was acting hyper-normal, a souped-up version of her former self. As I tried on the dresses she handed me, I looked in the mirror and saw me in a white dress with beige stripes, me in a white dress with doily-like lace, me in a pale pink dress with white flowers. I trooped out of the dressing room for my mother's inspection, dutifully turning this way and that at the wave of her hand while she nodded or frowned or shook her head.

I wondered what being beautiful had done for my mother other than give her no direction in which to gaze but into her own reflection. The state of being beautiful was indiscriminate; it was there for peasants and kings. You couldn't reclaim it for yourself. You could hide it under chador or veil, but it would be there still, more enticing for its secrecy. The state of being unbeautiful was a more exacting affair. If a man found you attractive, you knew it must be so, that he must have looked hard and long to see something within you and was not just another wistful aesthete panting after loveliness. I was suddenly glad I wasn't beautiful, that I didn't suffer my mother's misfortunes of vanity, her disappointment in how far beauty could get you, which was, in truth, not as far as one might imagine.

My mother decided on the pink dress. "White makes you look green," she said by way of explanation, holding out her credit card for the salesgirl to process. "This one is much more flattering. Makes you look thin."

I said nothing.

"My daughter is graduating high school next weekend," my mother told the salesgirl.

"Congratulations," the salesgirl said, smiling at me. She handed me the bag containing the dress.

"Thank you," I said, and swung the bag like a pendulum out the door.

That night I dreamed that Stephen was alive and grown, a gawky ten-year-old with too-big permanent teeth in the front and a cowlick in the back of his head. He was taking dresses from my closet and throwing them overhead, their diaphanous fabrics swelling and falling like parachutes. We were laughing together, looking up as they billowed down again, clothes floating, sailing, landing on our upturned faces. He seemed happy to be there with me, as he had been when he was alive. And I was happy too. We were two children delighted by the repetition of a silliness, flinging the voluminous material up in the air—organdy and silk, satin, chiffon and chintz—delighted at gravity for bringing back down upon us what we had tossed away.

Seeking Counsel

It felt weird to be in Rachel's house now that she and I were no longer friends. Everything that had seemed familiar, that I'd taken for granted—the trash bins crusted with bread dough, the stacked booster seats and wooden high chairs—took on a foreign aspect. I'd come to see Jerry, who himself looked strange to me, perched on the kitchen counter with his hands at his sides.

"You want my advice," he said, his warm brown eyes looking at me with unusual severity. "Drop it. I mean, she says she's giving him up, right? Which I don't really understand, but okay. So no need to tell anybody. Everything's set."

"You don't understand why she should give him up?" I asked incredulously.

Jerry shrugged. "I know it's a pain in the ass when someone

older comes across like they've got the wisdom of the ages, Isa, but there're some things you just learn with time and experience. And one of them is that marriage is tough, and happiness is hard to find, and so . . . I don't know. She's your mother, but try to see it from her point of view. From the point of view of a woman."

This stung a little. I thought I *was* a woman, and it irritated me that Jerry didn't see me that way. "So you think her cheating on my father is okay?" I said harshly.

Jerry stroked the counter behind him. His fingernails were dirty. When I showed up he'd been working in the garden. He'd hugged me and I smelled damp earth. "I don't know, Isa. Do I think it's okay? No, it's wrong. It's hurtful. Do I think it's human? Yes. People get lonely, they get disappointed—"

"Have you ever cheated on *your* marriage?" I said. Jerry's first wife had died after years of being sick with cancer. Audrey had told me of his devotion. He and Louise were always smiling at one another and calling each other "chum" and "baby."

Jerry smiled at me. "Listen, Isa," he said, "if you want to know what I really think, I think none of this is any of your business. Some things are private, even within families. You asked me what I think, and that's pretty much it. I don't pass judgment."

"But—"

"Life is hard and everyone's just trying to make their way."

To this I had no answer. I stared sullenly at the brick-colored linoleum, which was strewn with Cheerios and dog food.

"Isa?" Jerry said.

"Yeah?"

"We miss seeing you. Rachel hasn't said anything to us about what happened, but I'm sorry you're not close anymore."

I kicked at a Cheerio with the toe of my sneaker. "Yeah, well," I said.

"She's spending more time at her dad's these days," Jerry said. "It's a lot quieter over there, I guess. Less crazy."

I nodded.

"She's a good kid, Rachel," he said, "but it's been hard on her."

"I know."

"Hey, Isa?"

"Yeah?"

"Come by anytime. You're always welcome; you know that. Anytime. We'd love to see you."

I smiled. Jerry was pulling on his beard, which was grayer than when I'd first met him, and there were downcast wrinkles at the corners of his mouth. It made him look like a sad person, which I knew he was not.

"Okay," I said. "Thanks, Jerry."

He waved a hand in front of his face. *"De nada,"* he said. "Hey, next time you stop by, let's bake some bread!"

Irresolute

My father was tired when he got back from Berkeley. The experiment hadn't gone well, and there was tension between himself and the leader of the UC team. He seemed grouchy and preoccupied, which was just as well, because it gave me an excuse to keep out of his way.

We were studying *Hamlet* in AP English. The Prince of Denmark's dilemma sprang from the page to my own heart like all the slings and arrows of outrageous fortune. I didn't understand the controversy surrounding the interpretation of the play. It seemed perfectly straightforward to me. Ghost or no, Hamlet knew what he knew, and if he hesitated, it was only because it was hard to work up the nerve to exact vengeance, in any case, especially if it meant hurting his own mother. He knew that she loved Claudius and was, if not entirely innocent of suspicion, then merely weak, not evil.

It was the first week in June, and summer was testing its powers early. Temperatures were in the eighties and the air was slick with humidity. There was no air-conditioning at school. I signed out early to escape the embalming heat.

The truth was that I was doing very little at school these days except obsessively reading and rereading *Hamlet* for a final paper I was writing about the themes of incest and sexual passion in the play, which I knew would blow mild, bespectacled Mr. Keniston away. I should have been, as my father kept reminding me, keeping my grades up so that I would have a better chance of transferring from SUNY-Albany after my freshman year, but it wasn't happening. If anything, my grades had slipped into the grim, uncharted territory of the C range, and I didn't care. I had become obsessed with the idea of betrayal, with the fallibility of marriage and the charade of love. It felt to me, in some deep, obstinate way, that if my parents were no longer in love, if their marriage was more an obligation than a commitment to anything higher and truer, then this had profound ramifications for my whole existence. It meant that my birth had been a mistake, a glitch, that the mere breathing of air was something I didn't deserve. A quaint notion, and testament to how innocent I was, how idealistic, because, of course, if this were true, how many of us would feel comfortable about our portion of oxygen?

I walked home along the church path, stopping to smoke a cigarette at the white birch stump. I looked toward the church and wondered if it would make a difference if I were religious, as it had for Hamlet, who was concerned about his soul's everlasting torment. I had, as a child, been curious about religion, but my father was such a proponent of scientific skepticism that I had left unexplored what might have been a spectacular gift for credence.

I decided it would not have mattered much—a nihilistic Hamlet would probably not have hesitated quite so long—and what could zealous religious belief have possibly added to my own moral judgment?

When I got to the house, I noticed that my mother's car was in the garage. She was usually at BCC at this time of day, so I was mildly surprised, but I figured it must be awkward to have to face a professor with whom you had just called off an affair.

I opened the front door quietly, and I was almost immediately rewarded by the sound of my mother's voice talking urgently into the telephone in the kitchen.

"I know," she was saying. "I feel the same. But what can we do?"

There was a slight pause.

"I don't know, Bill," my mother said, this time with more anguish. "I love you, too."

I opened the door and slipped out again. I walked down our street, past the houses with the box lawns and the iron eagles and the flagpoles, and thought that perhaps if we had tried harder to maintain these small symbols, these conventions of Americana, we would have succeeded at being a more normal family. If my father had mowed the grass more often instead of paying a kid down the street to do a desultory job, if we'd put out the Stars and Stripes for those holidays that were deemed societally important, if we had planted marigolds or pansies on our walkway, put a spread-winged eagle, flat and black, over our front door—maybe any one or some combination of these things would have made a difference to the gods of the ordinary.

My mother could not give him up, this poet, this William R. Moulten. She had promised me she would, with tears streaming down her face, but she couldn't do it. You'd think this would have made me more understanding, the realization that my mother might not be able to help herself, that her unhappiness was so present that she must lose herself in whatever was available to her. But generosity did not reside in me. I walked around the block, hands deep in the pockets of my jeans, brooding over my mother's double betrayal, her persistence in this folly that was, for me, so grotesque I felt it reflected on my own dignity. I was soaked with sweat at this point, the back of my shirt clinging to me as though I had a sponge mop stuck between my shoulder blades.

I arrived back at the house with much slamming of doors and shuffling of shoes on the slate foyer, and found my mother off the phone, preparing my favorite, *mandu-guk,* for dinner.

Hypothetical

I said nothing to my mother about what I'd overheard. She was nervous. She dropped things at the dinner table, causing my father to snap at her.

"*Yeobo,*" he scolded, "what's the matter?"

"Nothing, *yeobo,*" she replied, wiping up the spills, bending to pick up the silverware.

He looked concerned as my mother went over to busy herself with the *mandu-guk.* "When was the last time you went to doctor?" he asked. "Maybe you should go for checkup."

"I'm fine, *yeobo,*" she said. "Just clumsy."

My father's eyes softened as he watched her ladle soup into the lacquered bowls. "It's not like you," he said huskily. "You are usually so graceful."

My mother pretended to be focused on the difficult task of assigning the right ratio of dumplings to broth in each bowl. I watched her false studiousness and felt the sweetness of my father's love. It was almost unbearable.

"Myung Hee, help your mother," my father said, and immediately, without resentment, I got up and took a bowl from my mother's hands. She shot me a warning look.

"Here you go, Dad," I said, presenting his bowl with two hands, in an exaggerated display of Korean politeness. He looked up at me, some of the softness carrying over from his vision of my mother. "Thank you, Myung Hee," he said. "Mmmm, this looks good!"

It was two nights later that I woke to the sound of my father going down the stairs in his slippers.

When I was younger, lying in bed at night, I imagined I was blind. I believed my sense of hearing became more acute as a consequence, reaching the radarlike proportions of a bat's. I would listen to the creaking of the house, my brother's middle-of-the-night feeding cries, a car turning down our street. The sound I would listen for was my father's ritual excursion downstairs. It was, in some strange way, the closest I felt to my father, these late nights when I was in bed and he was downstairs, unaware of my hyper-vigilance to his small sounds, the creak of the freezer door, the clink of ice in a glass.

I got up now and let my legs swing across the edge of the bed. I sat there for a moment, feeling cool air circulate around my feet, then stood up in one motion, like a gymnast landing a jump. I wore an oversized blue T-shirt with a picture of Daffy

Duck, which I'd had since I was thirteen; it was so comfortable, the cotton thinning to transparency in spots, the material the softest-feeling thing imaginable.

I crept down the stairs barefoot and stood for a moment in the kitchen doorway. My father was sitting in his customary spot, a glass of whiskey close at hand. The lights were out and there was no magazine in front of him. He seemed to be staring at the far side of the table. My eyes adjusted in the dark and I made some small noise in my throat to warn him of my presence.

"Myung Hee," he said hoarsely, "what are you doing up? It's late."

This made me smile—my father with his talent for stating the obvious.

"I couldn't sleep," I said.

He grunted. "You get from me," he said. "Not like your mother. World could be ending and she'd be sound asleep."

To my surprise, my father motioned toward the bottle of Jim Beam, which was still out on the counter. "Whiskey helps," he said. "Pour a small glass. Not too much. You are old enough."

I got out a glass and poured an inch into it, got two ice cubes, and dumped them in. I realized I should have done it the other way, that the sound I listened for was made by putting the ice in the glass first, then stirring the liquid to make the ice cubes tinkle.

I sat down beside my father and held the glass out level with my forehead. "Cheers," I said. My father touched my glass with his, tilting it slightly toward mine.

"*Ganpai,*" he said.

We drank. The whiskey tasted harsh and smoky, with a warmth going down that felt like velvet.

"Good?" my father asked. He seemed amused.

I nodded.

It was a companionable moment. We sat in silence for some time, sipping our drinks.

"Dad?"

"Mm?"

"As a scientist—hypothetically—if you knew that the result of some experiment was very exciting and made a lot of people happy, but you also knew the data was being falsified, would you feel obligated to tell, or would you let it go, knowing that the data was inaccurate but knowing it did no real harm?"

I'd spent a long time configuring this particular analogy, certain that this approach would catch my father's attention right away, but now that I'd spoken it aloud, it sounded forced and inapplicable to me. Of course I knew what he would say.

My father furrowed his brow, as he did when he was given a pleasing problem to consider. "So, someone is deliberately falsifying data to get this exciting result?" he asked.

I nodded.

"And yet you say this falsification does no harm? I find that difficult to believe. Any result not based in sound research does harm. We could say we had a cure for cancer, and that would make people happy, but if we had no hard facts, it would not cure cancer, and this would cause harm."

I tried a different tack. "But I mean in a more general way. Morally, say, if you know something is hurtful or harmful to another person, but they don't know it, so they think they're happy. Do you have an obligation to tell them, or is it better to keep quiet?"

My father pondered this for a moment. He stared at a spot on the table as though the answer could be gleaned there. "If a person thinks he is happy," he said slowly, "but this sense of happiness stems from ignorance of the true situation, then he cannot be truly happy."

"So, you think that if you are the only one who knows the truth, you should tell the person, even if it might make them unhappy?"

My father took a long pull from his drink, and I followed suit. There was a prolonged silence, no longer companionable.

"Myung Hee-*ya,*" he said, turning to look at me, "what are you trying to say?"

"Nothing," I said quietly. I was wishing for Hamlet's fine oratory, his slippery, brilliant soliloquizing that could turn the words back and around themselves, eluding suspicion, deflecting meaning.

"Obviously something," my father said. Anger had returned to his face, the familiar mask.

I knew two things in that instant: that he did not want me to tell him, and that he already knew but had decided to deal with it the same way he dealt with everything that was inconvenient or painfully unquantifiable—unsolvable for X or Y—by tamping the emotion down so hard and tight, the way he used to tamp his pipe tobacco, that there was no way to get at it without ignition.

I was angry now myself, though, for petty, shameful reasons. I felt my father wanted to protect my mother, the two of them content to remain aligned against me, with their shared language and their strange, inexplicable marriage. For almost my entire life I had not understood what my mother saw in my father, how she could stay with a man so severe. Recently, I'd come to wonder how my father could love my mother with such unwavering devotion, when she was so capricious and self-centered. I felt there was no loyalty in my mother except to herself, to some conception she had of her dazzling future, a destiny that had begun with a nearly lethal accident and that had shown itself only in comparable mockery since. Their intimacy baffled and annoyed me, and because I could not understand it, I was seized with the desire to destroy it.

"She's in love with her poetry teacher," I said. "The guy at BCC. I saw them together. I tried to get her to break it off, but she wouldn't."

My father said nothing.

"I'm sorry to have to tell you," I said, "but it's been going on a long time—whenever you're away—and I just think it's not fair for you not to know."

"You are sure?" my father said, as though confirming a calibration.

I nodded.

"This professor who wears blue jeans to class?"

"Yes."

"The one who tells students to call him Bill?"

"Yes."

My father's face was unreadable. He turned to his drink. Moments passed. I had finished my whiskey, having felt need of its courage long ago. It left a burn in the back of my throat.

"Dad?" I said after a time.

My father grunted.

"Are you okay?"

He looked at me as though I were crazy. "Am I okay?" he echoed. "With the thing you have just told me," he said, "you ask if I'm okay?"

"I'm sorry, Dad. I just really thought you deserved to know."

"Deserved?"

"I mean, you said yourself that a person who thinks he's happy but is ignorant of his true situation isn't truly happy," I reasoned.

My father was silent. He averted his face from mine. Finally he said, in a voice rough with pain, "I thought we were speaking hypothetically."

Watch

Walking out of school on the last day of classes, I ran into Rachel. Since the day she'd accused Hero of rape, we'd avoided one another. I didn't feel like we were angry at one another particularly, or that either of us harbored ill will. It was more like we were so embarrassed and confused by what had happened between us that we could barely stand to be in the same room.

"Hey, Isa," she said.

"Hey, Rachel," I said. "Can't believe we're finally out of here, can you? What a shithole. Still, it's hard to believe we're done." The stupidity of my words reverberated in my head like wind.

Rachel tipped her head to one side, a birdlike gesture, as

though she were trying to see me more clearly. "How've you been?" she said. "Jerry said you stopped by the other day."

"Yeah," I said.

"What are you doing this summer?"

I shrugged. I had an internship at the local paper and a part-time job slicing bologna at Price Chopper. "Nothing much," I said. "How about you?"

Rachel smiled, a genuine smile. Her eyes sparkled like chips of malachite. She'd had her hair cut, and it suited her, curled just beneath her ears. "I'm going to Italy with my dad and step-mom," she said, with such spontaneous enthusiasm that it made my heart sink. "We're going to Florence, Rome, and Venice."

"That's great," I said. It did sound great. I imagined Rachel eating pasta in some sidewalk trattoria in a Roman piazza, Rachel pacing the Uffizi Gallery, spellbound by Michelangelo.

"I should be earning money," Rachel said, "but my dad says he thinks going to Italy is a better intro to art school than flip-ping burgers at McDonald's."

I nodded dumbly. Not once in my life could I remember prefacing any remark with "My dad says . . ." The confidence it denoted, the sense of daughterly adoration. It was such an inno-cent phrase, so trusting. I stood there, corrosion in my chest, and nodded for an idiotic length of time, like one of those bobbing dolls from Korea that we had in our living room.

"Well, good luck," I said. "If I don't get a chance to talk to you at graduation, have a great trip and a great time at Cooper Union. I know you'll do really well."

"Good luck to you, too, Isa," she said. She started to walk

away, then turned partway back. "Uh, there's a graduation party at Dusty's house on Friday night if you want to come."

"Oh, what time?" I knew she was just being polite, but I was touched all the same.

"I don't know, things'll probably get started around nine, nine thirty."

"Thanks," I said. "Maybe I'll stop by."

"Good," she said, nodding. "Well, see you maybe."

"Yeah, see you." I had to turn away because I felt the salt sting of tears.

The night before graduation, my mother laid my dress out on the bed like she used to when I was in first grade. On the floor she put the pink sandals we'd bought to go with it.

"I hope it doesn't rain," my mother said. "So pretty, this dress, these shoes."

My mother had ironed my black graduation robe, which hung like a boneless carrion bird on the back of the closet door, along with the mortarboard with the green tassel that I knew disappointed my parents, who had expected me to wear the gold tassel of the National Honor Society.

The truth was that I'd come to loathe the pink dress with the large white flowers that seemed to creep from the back like a viral growth. Pink was not a color I felt an affinity for, and I was surprised by the dress, which I never would have consented to wear if I'd been paying attention.

"Wear stockings tomorrow," my mother said. "This color with your dress." She rummaged in my drawer and brought out a flat package. "And Isa, don't walk too fast. Let Daddy take your picture. And remember to smile, Isa. You always look so serious."

When Stephen died I'd felt silence spiral around our house like the thornbushes in a fairy story. Silence descended upon us once again after I told my father of his wife's infidelity. Only the quality of the silence was different. When Stephen had died, my parents were mute, literally shocked into speechlessness by the sudden and terrible way their son's life had ended. I looked to them with reverence and fear, struck dumb by their voicelessness, waiting to hear the reassuring sound of words, to have them explain Stephen's death in ways that would make sense to me, the way my father could explain how a water pump worked or what made the moon wax and wane.

This time I was the silent one. My mother chattered in a voice that was unnaturally high in pitch, alternately cheerful, cautious, and imploring—or not alternately but all at once. My father was quiet, but only marginally more than usual. I could tell by the way that they continued to treat one another, cordially, following routine a bit more formally perhaps, that my father had not confronted my mother and that my mother did not yet know I had told him.

When my mother left my bedroom, I cleared the dress from the bed and pushed the sandals back underneath it. There was a knock on the door, and my father came in. He entered my room so infrequently that, seeing him framed in the doorway, I was momentarily frightened. He looked haggard, tiny lines crosshatched into his face, the pouches under his eyes gray and slack. I thought of the plastic surgeon, Dr. Cheon, and his immaculate face, taut with unnatural smoothness, and how much better my father looked, despite the evidence of his age and sadness. It was a face that betrayed its history, of stoicism and pain, and the strenuous disavowal of emotion; the cost paid in the flinching corners of his eyes and the deep crease in his ridgelike brow. It seemed incredible to me that I had never noticed this before, how my father's face was not, in fact, like a mask, stern and concealing, but like a map, containing the roadways of his suffering.

"Myung Hee," he said, his voice hoarse from disuse. He had a small, narrow box in his hand, black with a gold bow. "We wanted to give this to you tonight. So you can wear tomorrow."

He handed me the box. I took it, the "we" conspicuous by my mother's absence from the room.

"Should I open it now?"

My father nodded.

I lifted the cover from the box. Inside was a gold Seiko watch with a delicate chain wristband.

"Look on back," my father instructed.

I took the watch out and turned it over.

For Myung Hee
6/11/76

was inscribed on the flat gold surface.

"Wow, thanks, Dad," I said. I wound the watch, and my father put up his own so I could see what time to set. I put it around my wrist and he reached over to do the clasp. He rarely touched me; the feel of his fingers against the inside of my arm was cool.

"It's beautiful," I said. I hugged him awkwardly. He leaned over and patted my shoulder.

"Okay," he said, straightening. "Big day tomorrow. Get good night's sleep."

It was the last time I saw him.

Conflagration

The night before graduation, I lay in bed, vaguely apprehensive and excited about the next morning. There were parties all over town. You could hear the squeal of tires as cars of revelers sped from one house to the next, an occasional cry of drunken exuberance fading into the night.

Rachel had invited me to Dusty's party, and I had thought about it but could not bring myself to go. When I saw Rachel, I could not help thinking about Hero and the night in the hotel room in Utah, which marked the closest I had felt to either of them, but also the moment we began to lose one another entirely. I remembered the weight of her arm on my hip, the way she'd kissed me on the mouth, her lips hot and sweet, tasting like cotton candy. I had loved her and she'd bewildered me, with both her response and her withdrawal.

If Rachel remembered, she gave no sign. She treated me, that day outside of school, like we had never stopped being friendly, but also as though we'd never been particularly close. "Hope to see you there, Isa," she had said, smiling that newly acquired, unironic smile, her voice similarly uninflected. She'd changed so much, this strange, grinning creature. But then, so had I. Only I couldn't help feeling that while Rachel had elected to change herself, simply by turning on a switch somewhere, I had had change foisted on me like the laying on of chains.

That night I did not wait for my father's cue, but crept downstairs sometime around midnight to pour myself a glass of Jim Beam. This was something I'd started doing at odd moments of the day and night, stealing a swig of gin or a mouthful of vodka. Just something to warm me and make my brain go dim. I was beginning to think that these persistent feelings I had—a loneliness that would not go away, a heartbreak that would not heal, a righteous anger that would not forgive—were not rites of passage, or hormonal changes, but permanent character traits that I would struggle with forever, the calcification of personality, a readied response to a world I had only recently come to know and mistrust.

I drank the whiskey neat, raising the glass to myself in a mocking congratulatory toast. As I sat at the kitchen table with my glass in the air, I felt a momentary confusion, as though I were my father—sitting at his place, drinking his whiskey, looking out into the dark, not in any true sense of thought or consciousness but in a way more of feeling—the Korean concept of *noon'chi*, which was like a gut instinct or hunch. I felt I knew what it was like to be my father, to be wakeful in the night in a country far from home, lost in memory, musing on a past that had accumulated most densely so long ago but that caught up to him here occasionally, under the cover of a foreign darkness.

He had tried to teach me, not about his personal past but about our collective history. "This is important, Myung Hee," he'd say. "It is your heritage. Aiee, how can I make you understand? Look at you!" He'd thrust out his hand, palm up, his face wildly disapproving.

"Okay, so the Yi Dynasty lasted until the Japanese occupation in 1909?" I'd say, parroting back something he'd said earlier.

"That's right, from 1400s to 1900s. That's why we speak of the *'han* of five hundred years.' You understand *han?*"

"That thing you say Koreans feel? Kind of like regret?"

My father twisted his mouth in frustration. "No real translation in English," he said. "It's a kind of sadness, or longing. A sense of loss. So much suffering, so much oppression. From China, Japan, from our own Korean kings and governments. Political corruption. Violence. Brutality. To understand Koreans, Myung Hee, you must understand this concept of *han*. We learned the hard way that one's individual will cannot overcome external forces. Some factors are too large, too overwhelming. You Americans don't feel this, I think."

"You say 'we Koreans' and 'you Americans.' Which am I?" I asked.

My father was caught off guard by the question. His brow furrowed as he regarded me for a moment. "Too soon to tell," he said. "Wait and see."

Now I rinsed my glass out, dried it with a towel, and replaced it in the cabinet. I went back upstairs and fell into what must have been an astonishingly deep, if not restful, sleep.

I dreamed that it was summer and Stephen and I were in the yard playing hide-and-seek. He stood next to Isatree, his hands over his eyes.

Then, in the strange, fluid logic of dreams, it was autumn and we were raking leaves into piles. I buried Stephen under the brown, dead mass, where he lay perfectly motionless. I enticed our parents over and he jumped out, laughing, hair adorned with debris, like a demented jack-in-the-box.

I smelled leaves burning on the curb. My father made us stand back as he brought the burning flame to the crackling piles. Stephen and I were mesmerized by the sweep and bend of the fire as it flared and was driven by the wind. Ribbons of orange entwined with black helixed upward and fell, the crackle and snap of twigs like tiny fireworks expelling sparks and jewel-like embers. Standing on one side with a clear view of the fire, we were suddenly teary-eyed with smoke.

I remember the solidity of my brother's body next to mine, standing there with the wind and the smoke and the immolating leaves. My father stood with the rake in his hand, one arm around my mother, who had a sweater around her shoulders and her arms hugged to her chest. We all looked into the fire, at the ridge of flame that lined the end of our yard.

My eyes began to burn with tears, from the smoke and the fire and the dried leaves that spiraled to ash in the hot air. I could no longer see Stephen standing next to me. I tried to open my eyes, but the smoke stung too harshly. I felt panic hit me, like that day in the elementary school woods, fear coming on like a seismic shaking. The smoke was entering my lungs now, cutting off my clean, unburdened breath. I shouted Stephen's name, but I was blind and choking and could not pursue him.

It took a tremendous amount of will to rise up from the bottom of that unbreathable, smoke-clogged drowning. It was as though sleep and fire conspired to weight me down, to hold me under that murky happiness. I coughed and woke. It took me several seconds to figure out where I was. I thought for a moment that I'd overslept graduation and that the heat I felt was a blazing noon.

I struggled to get out from under the bedsheets. The air in the room was dense and black. A figure appeared to stand beside me—I gave a lurch of fear—but it was only my graduation robe hunched on its hanger. There were loud snapping sounds, sirens, and voices outside my window. I went to the door, but it was hot. I stood there, coughing through my hand, too stunned to panic. I saw yellow flame licking the underside of the door, and it occurred to me that I should do something, but I didn't know what.

"Cover your face!" I heard a man yell, and then a crash, and an ax handle smashed through the window, shattering the glass and splintering the casement. I looked down and saw that I was on fire.

Survivor

I woke in the ICU. I say "woke," but it was more like a drifting in and out of wakefulness; I was heavily sedated and was being treated for smoke inhalation and severe burns on my legs. For a while I was plugged into a ventilator that made me feel like an elephant breathing through a reed.

After a week I was transferred to the adolescent wing of the burn ward. Doctors came and went, as well as nurses in blue uniforms with no hats, looking like girls at a pajama party. My sense of smell wasn't good, but I do remember jolting awake once to the odor of burnt popcorn wafting from the nurses' station.

On the eighth day they told me. My parents were dead, killed in the fire, which was still under investigation. The policeman who told me this was grim. He asked about next of kin, and I could only swallow stupidly, the back of my throat burnt and raw.

The fact of my parents' deaths didn't register at first. I must have been in shock, or maybe it was the opposite—maybe instead it held a terrible clarity. My high school class sent flowers, as did colleagues of my father's, and the contingent from Berkeley. Mrs. Williamson came briefly, with Mrs. Benoit and Mrs. Sanderson, standing with pitying looks on their faces, placing their Whitman's Samplers on the bedside table.

Pastor Park, of whom my father had been dismissive, visited every week. He would sit and read the Bible to me in Korean, from a book with pages as thin as rice paper. I marveled that the words from the other side didn't bleed into the words he read, wondering, as I listened to his fervent, cantabile prayers, if he was reading both sides of the page at once—some biblio-equivalent of speaking in tongues.

Jerry and/or Louise came every day, Jerry with loaves of rye bread in rumpled paper bags and jars of homemade jam and pickles. Louise brought a Plexiglas box filled with a thousand origami cranes in all colors that she and her after-school kids had made to wish me luck on my recovery. Rachel sent a postcard of Betty Boop, and Audrey sent me a get-well card from Binghamton, where she was studying music.

For weeks I could not speak. The doctors found nothing wrong with my vocal cords. Still, when I tried, I could manage only a rasping breath that sounded like the bleating of a sheep.

I had nightmares about the fire every night, but in the trans-figuration of dreams it was the fire of my mother's childhood that I dreamed of, the celluloid fire with the smell of kerosene and the crowded room of panicked children.

Sometimes my father would be cast in the role of the faithful servant, smothering the flames that danced on my mother's head like a crown of light, bending down to scoop her up in his arms. I would watch in the corner, my view obscured by smoke, thinking to myself that he would come back for me, that he would notice where I was and return. But he never came back, and like the *ajumma* whom my mother had described to me, I looked down to discover my dress ablaze, undulating with fire like a wave, lapping upward, more a drowning than a burning, if you could discount the singed odor and the overwhelming heat. While I burned I turned into one of the Christmas angels that revolved on our living-room coffee table when I was young, a small, fixed figure chasing after flame.

I woke from these dreams bathed in sweat, panting, the bedsheets twisted and kicked off the bed. Sometimes a nurse would happen along and try to comfort me, patting my forehead and making soothing noises as one would to a wounded animal; sometimes there would be no one and nothing except a sterile hospital room in moonlight, and I would lie back in bed and think how I deserved every nightmare, every disquieting memory, every terror and punishment.

I was listless, uncooperative, dangling like a rag doll when they tried to get me into the shower, slumping to the floor as soon as they let me go. Once when Pastor Park was in the room, reading from his transparent pages, I felt a hardening in my chest, an ingot of pure despair, to which his singsong assurances only added a gilded weight.

One day I went into the bathroom and looked at my face in the mirror. It was sallow, with chalky circles under the eyes. My lips were severely chapped and they parted with difficulty. I looked into the darks of my eyes and tried to say something to myself; I can't remember what—something like, "My name is Isa Sohn and my parents are dead"—but I couldn't manage the coordination of my mouth with my voice, and nothing came out but a dry croak.

Time passed slowly. I tried to keep to the surface of things. The linoleum floors. The concrete walls painted aquamarine. I learned the nurses on the ward. Abby and John, whom I liked. Norah and Kristen, whom I did not. When John was there, it was night. When Dr. Aukofer came in, it was morning. If Janelle, my roommate, was watching cartoons, it was Saturday. If Pastor Park appeared, it was Sunday afternoon.

The police report called it murder-suicide. My father apparently waited until my mother was asleep and then poured gasoline on and around the perimeter of the bed. I could imagine him, head bent to the task, meticulously meting out the contents of the red container with the yellow spout that was ordinarily kept in the garage.

I imagined my mother lost in sleep, the only one among us who had the gift for it, lying on her side, one arm slung over her head (the way she'd slept after Stephen died). I saw my father, in his blue pajamas with the white piping, getting into bed beside her, flicking a match, and spooning up tight, hugging her to him as the room ignited into a false dawn.

I believed this was what happened. There was no discussion,

no fight. My father simply made up his mind, for whatever reason believing that this simultaneous death was what was called for, the correct answer (*work not shown*) to this particularly difficult and complex problem.

People assumed I was mute from grief. They pitied me my sudden orphanhood. They recalled what had happened to my brother years earlier and understood my anguish to be only sensible given the devastation I'd suffered. *Such a tragedy,* they whispered. *Poor, poor girl.*

It *was* grief that drove me, just not the type they imagined. It was hard to believe my father capable of such a thing, harder still to think that telling him the truth about my mother should have unleashed such horror. I suppose I'd wanted him to punch William Moulten in the nose, or to pay my mother closer attention so she wouldn't go wandering off. Or maybe I was just still upset about Hero, and my own bitterness made me want to destroy my mother's pleasure, her—as Jerry had pointed out—not-so-horrible crime of taking happiness when it came her way.

But what hurt most deeply was something much more selfish. My father had given me a new watch, the only present I can remember receiving from him, and then gone off to kill my mother and himself. Didn't he consider that the fire would probably kill me too? On the eve of my graduation from high school?

I don't think he meant to kill me. I don't think he thought about me at all. Once again my father's attentions had settled on my mother, his ministrations, loving or malevolent, focused entirely on her. I was irrelevant, a mere by-product of his obsessive love, to the end the outsider in the threesome. Not the one who survived, but the one who was left behind.

Tall Ships

Three weeks after the fire, the nation celebrated its bicentennial. Abby brought me a blue-frosted cupcake with a flag stuck on a toothpick. We watched the fireworks over the tall ships on TV.

"They're so beautiful," Abby said. Silhouetted against New York Harbor the ships were tall, stately, and sleek, but they looked strangely haunted, also—ghostly in full sail, skeletal with bare masts. An armada of the majestic dead bobbing in dark water.

What can I say about the time I spent on the burn ward? That it was gruesome, that it was tedious, that it was not so bad. I am grateful to so many people I met there, to Abby and John; to Dr. Aukofer and his burn team; to Mike, my psychiatric social worker; to Helen, the volunteer who wheeled the book cart; to Janelle, my roommate and the bravest person I ever met; to Clive and Andy in PT, who tortured me in ways I'd thought were outlawed by the Geneva Conventions.

The truth is that I quickly grew comfortable there. It began to feel like home. Yet when I think back on the time I spent there, it's like seeing through a veil; much of what I remember is clouded by painkillers and, when they weren't working, by the pain itself, which was like a heavy blanket that gave neither warmth nor comfort.

Some moments I remember clearly, the veil suddenly pulled aside, the way Dr. Aukofer pushed the curtain back when he was done examining my burns. Most of these moments were unpleasant, like the first time my wounds were debrided. Or those times I would rise up out of Percocet-induced unconsciousness, the reality of my situation hitting me like a brick to the head.

Everyone said I was brave because I didn't complain. When they hurt me with needles and bandages, I would close my eyes and count to ten. Sometimes tears would run down my face, but I would not cry out. I don't think I fully accepted the fact that I was alive. Meaning I did not believe it, did not wish for it. I felt like one of those tall ships among the choking crowds of well-wishers and tourists. The rockets' red glare, the fireworks bursting in air; this was life, the stuff of celebration, bright and boisterous—while I felt like one of the vessels below, drifting through from a darker century, spare and serious as a plague.

Rule of Nines

According to the Rule of Nines, I am burned over thirty-six percent of my body. They divide the body into parts, each nine percent of the total body surface area (TBSA). An arm counts nine percent, a leg eighteen. It's a tidy system. The charts they use are of a body sectioned off by dotted lines, like the ones drawn on posters of cows to show the cuts of meat.

There's a patch about five by six centimeters across my right thigh, and one slightly smaller along my calf. On my left leg, there is a blaze that runs from my outer thigh to the back of my knee.

I won't pretend that it isn't painful, excruciating, like heated knives cutting into you, and then this crawling sensation like ants eating you from the inside. When they change the dressings, or try to clean the wounds, it feels like I am being burned all over again. And even now, the itching can get so intense that it becomes painful, like a hundred bees stinging me.

But thirty-six percent is nothing. My roommate, Janelle, caught her hair on fire leaning to blow out the birthday candles on her fourteenth birthday. She's at eighty-one percent, mostly on her face and neck. Her left ear is just a hole at the side of her head, and after seven skin grafts, her face still has the texture of raw, stringy meat.

The skin is our largest organ. In adults, it averages more than two square yards. Imagine it spread out in one thin layer, bald, irregular parchment, like a ragged map of the body. It's the boundary wall between all we are and all we are not; our defense against all manner of assailants, visible and microscopic. It is the container of our corporeal selves and the vessel for our ethereal ones. When it burns, the border is breached, and we're suddenly permeable, undefined and undefended.

A strange paradox: after a severe burn, the body manufactures collagen to form scar tissue atop the injured area. The new surface is thicker and harder than normal skin. It has the look and feel of rope. Yet a healed scar is twenty percent weaker than the skin it replaces. It's more sensitive to air currents, to heat or cold, and even to touch. Which means, I suppose, that despite appearances to the contrary, I've grown more thin-skinned.

Trick Candles

One of my happiest moments on the ward was when I turned eighteen. Abby made a chocolate cake with Cool Whip frosting and HAPPY 18TH BIRTHDAY, ISA written in loopy red icing. John, Helen, and Janelle, and the kids on the ward, waited while Abby and I cut pieces of cake and scooped out ice cream. Dr. Aukofer came in, and the cardiologist, Dr. Carlo.

"Happy birthday, Isa," Dr. Aukofer said, swooping down to give me a kiss on the cheek. He handed me a present wrapped clumsily in silver paper. It was a copy of *Siddhartha* by Hermann Hesse.

"I loved this book when I was your age," Dr. Aukofer said, tapping the cover. I smiled. It had been one of Hero's favorites.

Abby gave me a powder-blue scarf that I'd seen her knitting

on the ward. "It's the wrong season, I know," she said, "but I wasn't sure how long it'd take."

Janelle gave me a book of crossword puzzles; John presented me with a Hohner harmonica—a "mouth organ," the box called it—in the key of C.

"Hey, Isa, make a wish and blow out the candles," Dr. Aukofer said, after Abby brought in the cake and they'd all sung "Happy Birthday" in disastrous harmony.

"Not too close," warned Janelle.

I closed my eyes and blew out the candles, and what I wished for was for everything to stay the same. It was not so much that I wanted to stay on the burn ward forever, though the thought didn't horrify me as it once had; it was more that I just wanted to pause. Something about that particular tableau—everyone relaxed and smiling, leaning in to watch me blow out the candles—made me feel it might be restful, to perch inside the moment like a bird on a ledge.

When I opened my eyes the candles had sprung alight again. Everyone was laughing at the joke of it, at my continued, vain efforts to blow them out. The candles would extinguish for a moment and then flare into flame again, over and over. And I laughed louder than anyone, because I had gotten my wish.

Accommodation

In the end they didn't know what to do with me. I still needed regular monitoring, but it was clear I didn't need to stay in the hospital. It took a long time, but Pastor Park was finally able to get hold of my mother's sisters in Seoul. There were five of them, married to industrialists and government bureaucrats. They harbored no apparent affection for my mother, whom I imagine they perceived as odd and undutiful. My mother had hardly mentioned them, except occasionally to warn me against their examples. *"Ayoo, Isa, don't make that face; you look just like my sister Hae Ja!"* *"My sister Hae Soo ate too many* mandu, *Isa; belly swelled up like a pig's."*

None of them wanted much to do with me. Impracticalities aside—they didn't speak English, I didn't speak Korean; I couldn't move to Korea, they couldn't move here—I don't think any one of them relished taking on the American-born daughter of their prodigal sister. *Halsu-eopseoyo. No way.* They sent me money to assuage their consciences, and this was fine with me.

Pastor Park and his wife offered to take me in, but their house in Scotia was tiny, and despite the ivory Cadillac, they had problems making ends meet. The memory of living with Mrs. Park for a week was still harrowing enough for me to refuse, borrowing the standard Korean excuse I'd heard my parents use many times. "Thank you so much," I said, shaking my head. "You are too kind, but I couldn't possibly let you go through so much trouble on my account."

Jerry settled it by suggesting I come live with him and Louise temporarily. All the kids were away at college now except Gary, who was in the fourth grade.

"I talked to Rachel. You can have her room. It'll be perfect. Louise and I miss having a teenager in the house." Jerry raised an eyebrow and smirked at the patent falseness of this last statement.

I nodded, my eyes filling with tears.

Jerry patted my arm. "Of course, you'll be expected to earn your keep," he said. "Can't have any loafers hanging around." He winked. "Except the ones we bake."

I groaned. It was the kind of very bad near-pun Jerry was always making, the kind that mortified his son and daughters and caused them to throw things at him.

"Thanks," I said. I had only recently started speaking again, and my voice sounded untrustworthy to me, dry and prickly in the back of my throat.

"*De nada,*" said Jerry, and he went off to make the arrangements.

Damage

So I came to reside at Rachel's. It was different, of course, with Rachel, Audrey, and Adrienne gone. The three cats, Cutie, Darling, and Princess, still prowled the premises, fat and indifferent, but Domino had been hit by a car the previous winter. Much of the vitality had seeped out of the place. It was no longer as frantic or as messy. I went down to the basement to watch soaps or game shows, enticed by old smells of must and stale pot. I found a peace symbol key chain that had belonged to Dusty, more than a dollar's worth of change, and an unused condom in the folds of the couch. Gary, who now ruled the basement, had added a miniature pool table, a small trampoline, and *Donkey Kong* on the TV.

I was supposed to be figuring out what I was going to do with myself.

"Take your time. No hurry," Jerry assured me.

"You're such a big help with the kids," said Louise, who paid me for helping her with the day care. "I'm lucky to have you."

I deferred admission to SUNY-Albany until the following fall, but I wasn't sure I wanted to go. A lot of money from my parents' savings had gone toward hospital bills, and I felt like I needed a job. The problem was I wasn't ready. I still had nightmares, and my legs were often in enough pain that I couldn't walk or even stand for long periods of time. Although I'd started speaking again, I found myself, even in the simplest situations, strangling on my own words, unable to articulate the rote expressions every five-year-old knows.

About a week after I moved in, while Jerry and Louise were out, I walked around the block to the spot where my house had stood. It was marked off by yellow caution tape—a black hollow of ground with the charred remains of metal and wood. There was a NO TRESPASSING sign in the yard; beside it another sign, WORK BY BARNETT & SONS, CONSTRUCTION, but there was no evidence of work being done.

I hadn't expected to walk so far, and my right leg (the more badly burned of the two) started to shake so violently I sank onto the curb. I was hoping Mrs. Williamson wasn't looking out her window just then; I didn't want to attract sympathetic attention. But looking at where the house had been for the first time since the fire, I was overcome.

I felt like a bead of oil on water, sliding along the surface precariously, without purchase. I could still remember all the rooms in that house—the way the kitchen was off the foyer to the right, and the staircase to the left led to the living room, and on up to four bedrooms and a bath. There was a newel post on the landing with a wooden ball perched on top that fit beneath my open palm. It was so hard and immoveable, that ball, embedded in the rectangular post that was planted somewhere under the carpet and the floor below. I believed in its permanence, and it, in turn, had persuaded me of my own.

But the newel post and the landing, the living room and the bedrooms, every feature and fixture of that house was gone, burned to the ground in about ten hours.

My legs throbbed and I felt unsteady, but I got up and walked slowly back toward Rachel's house. I was angry at myself for having come to look, rubbernecking at the scene of my own tragedy. I was angry because the image I'd held of our house, the solidity of it in my mind, had been replaced by this picture of ruin, and try as I might, I could not regain the house.

Correspondence

I read all the time at Rachel's. Louise took me to the library and I came back with ten books, the maximum allowed, and read them all in three weeks. They were mostly old novels—I liked French and Russian best—and biographies of writers, like Faulkner and Virginia Woolf, which I found bracing and instructive. I also read all I could find on severe burn injuries and their treatment, mostly so I could ask Dr. Aukofer questions at our biweekly appointments.

Occasionally there was mail for me. I got my diploma from IHS—a cream-colored piece of paper bordered in green with my name on it in Old English calligraphy and the stupid seal with an Indian in profile. Abby sent me a letter saying how much everyone missed me on the ward; John had scribbled on the bottom, wanting to know how the harmonica playing was going.

Rachel sent me cards, things she'd found in secondhand bookstores, black-and-white photos of the Brooklyn Bridge and the Empire State Building, taken in the 1940s. She scrawled a few sentences on the back that I mostly couldn't read. Something about a guy she'd met who took her to Harlem. Something about taking an art class with an old friend of Jackson Pollock's.

One day I got a letter from Hero, forwarded from the hospital. Louise handed it to me from a stack of mail she'd been looking through; the postmark was two months old. I took it down into the basement and read it by the flickering light of the television screen with the sound turned down. It surprised me how sweaty my hands were, opening the envelope, how hard my heart pounded. After all that had happened, you'd think I would have been immune. I'd come to think of Hero as a childhood playmate, someone whom I had played with in a sandbox when I was six, or been forced to buddy up with at recess. That he had been my first lover no longer seemed plausible to me. Or, in truth, that I'd had any lover at all.

The letter was written on a single sheet of paper ripped out of a spiral notebook. I read it twice before I realized that what was written there was not going to change.

Dear Isa:

My parents told me what happened. I'm so sorry. I wanted to come visit you in the hospital but the Unit nixed that idea. Not sure what their problem is. (When am I ever?) I hope that you're fine now. It sounds like you're gonna be.

I'm enjoying school a lot more than I thought I would. Living away from home is great, and being with a lot of kids with sight issues is kind of cool. I started a new band down here called Bare Aspirin. Sort of Velvet Underground type stuff. I think you'd really dig it. I've been writing lots of new songs. Maybe I'll send you some.

So, have you read any good books lately? (Ha, ha.) I've recently discovered Ayn Rand. You should really read *The Fountainhead,* Isa. It's brilliant. She believes that no one really acts altruistically, because even the desire to be altruistic is, at the core, selfish. And if we all just act on our own selfishness, we will actually be more productive and creative as a society. She says that's why capitalism works. Interesting stuff. You should definitely check it out.

I'm going to Rutgers starting next month. Wanted to go to Yale or Brown, but the fools didn't let me in! Oh well, I'm excited. I wonder where you'll be going. The Unit didn't say.

Anyway, I'm truly sorry about what happened with your folks. It must be tough. I wish that we were still close, but my own stubborn attitude got in the way, I guess. You're a cool kid, Isa, and I know you'll be just fine.

Love and headin' on down the road,
Chris

(Yeah, I know, using my middle name now. No one calls me Hero down here, and Herold is just too square.)

It was nice of him to write, I thought. This was precisely what Louise had said. "It's so nice of Hero to write, Isa. I saw his mother the other day, and she said he was leaving for college soon. You should write him back."

I knew I wouldn't, though. Some silences were recoverable and others weren't, and it seemed to me infinitely false to pretend one was when it was not.

I thought about Hero, tried to conjure his luminous body. I'd been reading in the burn literature that skin color is created by cells in the epidermis called melanocytes. When the skin is deeply burned, melanocytes are destroyed, and pigmentation defaults to an unprotected, pearlish white. The burns on my legs are this color now, with pink scars seizing up in the middle like the root system of a tree. It occurred to me that I had, in these specific spots, become albino.

I fed Hero's letter to a Bic lighter I found in Louise's purse, letting the ashes fall into the sink, where I watered them into the disposal. It wasn't bitterness I felt, though there was cause for bitterness. Hero's letter was a little too breezy to assuage either my longing or my curiosity. Ayn Rand and the Velvet Underground. I did not recognize the person I had loved, and I suppose I was getting used to this, so what I felt was a kind of hollow familiarity, a reverberating echo that was both dense and empty.

Love and headin' on down the road. Chris.

At least I had the satisfaction of knowing no one would ever again call him Hero.

Cowbird Egg

They all came back for Thanksgiving—Adrienne from Potsdam, Audrey from Binghamton, Rachel from Cooper Union. They seemed older, more sophisticated—Adrienne with her plucked eyebrows and angular haircut, Audrey in a long suede vest fringed with sheepskin, Rachel, arms drenched in silver bracelets, with kohl-rimmed eyes and iridescent eye shadow like dragonfly wings.

Rachel, in particular, seemed changed. She had acquired an abrupt laugh, and her face had taken on a tight, skeptical expression that seemed citified to me, part attitude and part affliction. She insisted on staying in the guest room. "It's your room now," she said, coming into her bedroom to get some clothes. She waved her hand like a monarch. "I don't live here anymore."

We hung out in the basement again, like old times. They talked about their lives away at college, stories about drunken escapades and boyfriends, and professors who were vindictive and only gave A's if you slept with them. Rachel talked about the City, and how from the window of her bedroom she could look out on a hundred windows, and how once she saw two men making love bent over a chair, and once a woman doing yoga in the nude. She talked about painting and the importance of light, and the whole time her hands sketched, across her pants leg, in a small journal, in the air with her cigarette smoke.

I played "Yankee Doodle Dandy" for them on the harmonica, a breathy, wheezing rendition that I'd been working on since I left the hospital.

"That's great, Isa," Audrey said doubtfully.

"You should try something from Dylan," said Rachel.

Back among them I felt like a usurper, the cowbird's egg hatched in the robin's nest (the way I'd felt riding home on the bus the afternoon Stephen died). Though I had gone through the most in the last few months, I looked the least changed (not counting my burns, of course, which were hidden beneath my jeans). My face was still broad and sallow, with a mouth that slanted to the left in a smirking, judgmental way; I had the same haircut. It seemed wrong that I should live here now, while Rachel and the others came back only to visit.

No one seemed to question what I was doing there, but no one asked what I'd been up to, either. They didn't inquire about my exploits on the burn ward, or my experience with fire and its aftermath; though Rachel, unable to control her curiosity, asked me to show her my burns, and when I did, self-consciously pulling down my pants, she winced but did not turn away.

"They look kind of cool, actually," she said. "Braided. Like a weaving or something. Do they hurt?"

"Not right at the moment," I said. "A little tingly, maybe. They're sensitive to the air."

I remembered how fascinated Rachel had been when I'd described my mother's burn, and I wondered if this was the morbid curiosity of the artist. I remembered our last night in Utah and pulled my pants up.

"Freak show's over," I said.

Rachel smiled at me. "It's never over, Isa," she said—maniacally, I thought. "That's the beauty of it."

Ping

One morning at the day-care center, Sadie Jersid greeted me with a book in her hand, the one about the duck that gets left behind on the Yangtze River. She's five years old, with sad brown eyes and black hair falling to her shoulders. Sadie liked the part where all the ducks got spanked, and was scared when Ping almost got eaten.

"That's not smart," she said, when Ping got caught.

She sat on my lap and we read the book through. When we were done Sadie turned the book over to the front and placed her flat palm on the cover.

"*'The Story About Ping,'*" she said, pretending she was reading. She traced the yellow duck with her index finger.

I brought my face closer to hers. Her hair brushed my mouth.

"Ping," I whispered into her ear.

She looked back at me.

"Ping," I said, one staccato syllable.

Sadie reached back to stroke my face. "Ping," she said, giggling.

Effects

In the beginning of December I received a parcel from SUNY-Albany, a large cardboard box wrapped in brown paper, tied with twine. Inside was an accordion file bulging with papers, an address book, and a short note from Cora, the secretary of my father's department. She'd been cleaning out my father's office, she said, and couldn't bear to throw out his files, so she'd sent them to me. She thought I was the one who should go through them. She was terribly sorry, she said, for my loss, and hoped that I didn't mind her sending along my father's effects.

My father's effects. This sounded funny to me. As though the effects my father had had could be mailed in a box. I pulled some stray papers from the file and was startled to see my father's handwriting again, those bold vertical lines so meticulous and certain. There were copies of old exams, lecture notes, grade books from 1972 (*Arnold, William; Astin, G. Humphrey; Barber, James*); dry-cleaning bills; pale green guest checks from Marie's Café, ringed with coffee stains; a couple of keys that looked like they went to a filing cabinet; torn-out articles from scholarly magazines; and a copy of a take-out menu from a Chinese restaurant near campus. One scrap of paper, ripped from the bottom of a newspaper, contained these words: "WD-40, lightbulbs, C batteries."

It overwhelmed me with proof of my father's life, as though I'd discovered he was hiding somewhere and had only staged his demise. I was surprised at the untidiness of the folder, its mundane contents. These were not the kinds of things my father attached himself to, or, anyway, they were not things I attached to him.

I found my father's university ID tucked into the file. His face stared out at me from the laminated photograph, a solemn man with dark glasses and a high, pale forehead, his thinning hair slicked down atop his head. This man, I thought, was my father. I put everything back inside the box and pushed it under Rachel's bed.

Lucky

At night I rubbed lotion on my burns, gently probing the uneven surface of the skin. It seemed to me like the terrain on the moon. I imagined a moon buggy, its tractor treads laboring to climb a lumpen clod of lunar ground.

I wore jeans all the time now, even though my scars were itchy and chafed against the denim, and when I was alone I couldn't help staring at myself, at the strange hideousness that had attached itself to me. Also, the donor sites on my backside, where they took pieces of skin to graft onto my legs, were healing in a kind of patchwork of pinks and reds. I wondered who would ever touch these places. Who would want to. And it was hard not to give over to self-pity.

"You're a very lucky girl," Dr. Aukofer had said to me in the hospital. "Your burns are confined to three isolated spots on your legs that will be fairly easy to conceal. Given the nature of the fire, you're lucky not to have been burned more extensively. You're lucky to be alive."

"Lucky to be alive." This was the refrain I heard from all sides, the chorus of well-meaning voices that crooned conspiracy by my bedside like a lullaby hush.

I closed my eyes and brushed my fingertips along the rough, damaged skin, and I thought, *Lucky.*

Discovery

Two weeks after it arrived, I took the box out from under Rachel's bed. I went through my father's files systematically, straightening the crumpled checks from the coffee shop, putting aside the grade books, aligning the loose pages of his notes so they made a neat stack. I threw away the Chinese menu and the academic articles; dropped the keys and my father's badge into a small manila envelope. Staring at the mimeographed exams my father had made up, the equations with Greek letters, subscript numbers, parentheses and brackets, I was like an archaeologist regarding some ancient, sacred text, puzzling over sentences I could not parse. My father seemed to reside within them. He felt nearby. The back of my neck grew hot, as though he were breathing close behind.

While I was going through test booklets—glancing at my father's "minus fives" ringed in fiery red that seemed to all but obliterate the timid, penciled offerings of his students—I came across a blue booklet filled with his handwriting. It took me a moment to register what it was, this thin booklet in my hand, its pages lined with dark letters, straight as chess pieces. It spooked me, like hearing his voice would have. I had to read slowly, a couple sentences at a time, and then I looked up into Rachel's bedroom—at the plaid bedspread and the paisley wallpaper—and I felt lost, amnesiac. When I had read it through, I began again.

Noona—

After all these years I still think of you every day. I do not know if you are alive or dead, if you died in 1950, or later. If you are alive, do you have children? You would be forty-four. I wonder how war changed you.

I live in the U.S. now, *Noona*. I am professor at State University in Albany, New York. I drive a big American car to work—a Buick. I come home to a nice house with a yard and big trees. My wife, Chung Hae Kyoung, who is from *yangban* family, dresses in latest Western fashions. We have one daughter, Myung Hee, who is completely American. We had a son, Myung Hwan, who, sadly, passed away at age four.

And even after all this, I feel time reversed, like my life here is the memory, and what is real to me is the smell of boiling *chig'ge* in the dirt kitchen of Chongwoondong, our mother scolding us for not wearing slippers, or even the field of rocks when I went back to Seoul and could not find where our house once stood.

Ah, *Noona*! So many men died. A quarter of my high school class. I think now what a waste of life. And for what? For the same result. The country divided as it had been at the beginning. Nothing changed except four million dead. And the question I ask is can you really live after you have seen so much death? I thought with Hae Kyoung it might be possible.

But it turns out I was wrong. Death followed me here. History followed me here. I have begun to see that I, too, am a casualty of war, that I died in the steep pass at Chirisan, on the beach at Yangyang, on the dusty road to Pusan at Daekwolyung. Four million times I died. Everything since has been happening to a ghost.

Noona—

When I think of the last day I saw you, I think of a head of *baechu* cabbage. There was still some food in the markets, and *Omma* wanted cabbage to make summer *kimchi*. It was a week into the war and we still believed it would end soon.

I had been in a fistfight with a schoolmate. I punched him in the nose with a right hook and sent him sprawling on the road. Ordinarily this might not have angered *Omma* so much, but she was nervous about the Communists, who were rounding up workers for their factories, and soldiers for their armies in the north. She was so afraid that they would take away her only son. She made me stay in and copy out "I will not fistfight in the road" a hundred times in my notebook.

I did not want to tell her why I hit that boy. It was because he teased me about having no father. He said because I lived only with women, I was becoming a woman myself. You know how *Omma* always starched my school uniform so stiff and shiny, and ironed my pocket handkerchiefs into creased squares.

I remember sitting in my room copying "I will not fistfight in the road." To relieve the boredom, I would copy the sentence in different handwritings, starting from the bottom word to the top, then going back down again. I kept listening to the sounds of chickens scuffling in the dirt outside and running water from the pump. It was quiet because many people had fled, but I could still hear the sound of fighting in the distance. I could hear your shuffling steps as you crossed back and forth from the kitchen to the courtyard, and then you were at the window.

"Tae Mun-ee," you called to me, low so our mother wouldn't hear you. "I'm going to market now to buy cabbage for *Omma.* I will try to bring you back something."

"Some caramel candy from end-of-the-road *ajasi?*" I asked.

You laughed. You knew these were my favorite. "I'll try," you said, and hurried out.

· · ·

The boy I punched in the nose, Lee Whangook, saw what happened. He ran to tell us. *Omma* broke down screaming, and I jumped up from my room and ran outside. Lee told me that a big truck had stopped. Two men got out and started talking to you. You tried to ignore them, but they grabbed you and pushed you into the back of the truck, where there were many others guarded by soldiers with guns. "You are pretty," Lee overheard one of them say. "If you're a hard worker, maybe I'll marry you myself."

Lee swore he heard the whole thing, hiding behind the corner. You said your mother was sick, that she needed you, but the men told you to be quiet, and the truck drove off.

I ran down the road, my shoes pressed down at the heels like a crazy person, shouting, asking the few people I met if they'd seen you. One old woman, dressed in the white *hanbok* of mourning, simply pointed north.

My Aunt

My father had mentioned his sister to me only a few times. He told me that she had the smallest feet and hands of any woman he'd ever seen. He'd cup his own hands together to indicate their tininess. He told me that she was the favorite of every street vendor and shopkeeper in the neighborhood, that she was clever and pretty and always hid her mouth behind her hand when she laughed. He told me that she loved peaches, and that her favorite color had been green. It was my mother who told me that she'd been killed in the war, along with my grandmother.

Noona—

A month after you were taken, *Omma* and I were eating dinner—rice porridge with *kimchi*—sitting at the small lacquer table, listening to the sounds of the war around us that were sometimes far off, sometimes close enough to shake the floor. I was wearing my old school uniform. *Omma* thought it would keep them from drafting me— as if either side cared about schooling!

When she had finished her meal, *Omma* balanced her chopsticks on the rim of her bowl. Pressing a hand to her chest, she burped; her dyspepsia had grown worse with the stress of the war. She took her napkin and, holding it to her mouth, burped again, crumpling the napkin delicately into a ball by her place.

"*Omoni,* are you okay?" I asked. She looked pale, and I noticed she was sweating.

She muttered something and got up from the cushion.

"*Gwaenchana,*" she said brusquely.

Omma went across the yard to the outhouse. I sat at the table and sipped the remains of rice-sweetened water. I was always hungry in those days; there was never enough to eat, and I wouldn't allow *Omma* to give me her portion of food. She had been gone some minutes, and I was just beginning to wonder whether I should go out and knock at the outhouse door. Remember the time she fainted in there and down-the-road *ajasi* had to cut out the bottom of the door? I got up and took two steps into the courtyard when there was a crack of light and a whooshing sound. I remember a flash, and a pain in the back of my head, then nothing. When I came to, our next-door neighbor, Mrs. Kang, was screaming and wailing and slapping my cheek.

"Aiyee!" she screamed. "You poor thing, get up! Are you hurt? Is anything broken?" Then, seeing that I was all right, just dazed, with a goose egg at the back of my head, she started crying again. "*Aigo,* you poor boy! You're an orphan now!"

Where the outhouse had been was now a smoking black crater with splinters of wood and a smell of sulfur. I looked into the crater, and around the charred ground, but there was nothing there. It was as though *Omma* had vanished from the earth. I am sorry to have to tell you, *Noona,* so many years later. *Omma* would have been embarrassed. But we cannot choose how we die.

Noona—

I wanted to tell you about the first man I killed. It was in the coastal city of Yangyang on the East Sea. We'd just retaken it from the North Koreans, and I remember we took down their flag with the red star and put up the *taeguki*. An icy Siberian wind blew sand from the beach into our eyes and noses.

I had to urinate, so I went a little way out to the dunes, not too far because there were land mines. I had been holding it for some time because it was too cold to pee, and I was scared. So I held my rifle out and had my finger on the trigger, even as my fly was down and I was pissing on the ground. It was then I saw him, crouching behind a knoll. I saw only his right shoulder and arm, and from where I stood I could detect the tension in his muscles where he gripped his rifle. I waited and he waited; he saw me, but he didn't know that I saw him. Even with the wind and the snow and the cold, I could feel the sweat down my back.

He stood up and I was paralyzed. He pointed his rifle at me. He was a boy of no more than sixteen, with flared nostrils and red apple cheeks. It looked like he'd grown up on a farm. There was no hatred in his face, only fear. I wanted to walk over and greet him. *"Jingu,"* I wanted to say. *Friend.*

But of course I didn't. Instead, he shouted and fired, but nothing happened. So I shot, and he looked down, and we could both see a hole open up in his chest, high up toward his throat, and the blood that splashed out across the snowy grass and sand. His body collapsed and fell to the side.

I knew two things in that instant, *Noona.* That I could kill a man, and that I was no killer. It was wartime and I was a soldier and my job was to fight, but I did not, like Lim and some of the others, enjoy it. I would not keep souvenirs of my kills—ears on a string, dog tags, ID cards. I would not boast about this in the tents later, or in the bars when we went home on leave. It is a terrible, sickening thing, *Noona,* what war does to a man. What it does to a boy who is only just becoming a man. Even now, over twenty years later, it breaks my heart to think of it.

Afterward I tried to bury him, but the wind kept blowing the sand away and the best I could manage was a shallow grave. In his pocket I found four crumpled one-won notes, a pocketknife, and a gum eraser. Also, his school picture, in a black uniform with a black cap, his name written on the back. "Kwak In Ho." He looked like the kind of boy I might have made fun of, with his crooked, hopeful smile and eyes that turned down at the corners as though he were sleepy. I put the picture on the sharp end of a stick and planted it by his head.

It turned out his rifle had jammed because it was clogged with sand.

The letters seemed to end there. I skimmed empty pages with blue-ruled lines. But then there was this, on the last page of the booklet, written in different-colored ink—blue ballpoint instead of black felt tip—in an uncharacteristically loose, sloppy hand.

The truth is, more and more these days, I feel as though I died in 1953—along with so many classmates and friends—and that everything that's happened since is a dream. America is a country without death. Everything is shiny and new to make you forget such a thing exists. Here people my age dress and act like teenagers. My wife does this. No one wants to be old. Why would they? There is no past here. There is no history. And here I am, a man trapped in the past, entangled in history, wandering like a ghost.

There is something strange these days with Hae Kyoung. I don't know what to think of it. Lately I feel she has changed. She had some trouble after our son, Myung Hwan's, death. She was in the hospital many times. Too much feeling, too much grief. Twice she tried to kill herself, but luckily both times I was able to prevent her. She is a passionate woman, and I love her very much. There is something about her that glows, a light inside. I think everyone must see it. I love her and yet sometimes I worry that it is not enough for her. Or maybe it is too much, it overwhelms her and I feel she must go away from me. Lately I am afraid

Excavation

It ends in midsentence, as though he'd been abruptly called away. I imagine my father in his office, receiving a phone call from a graduate student, a favor to ask, a form to sign. I picture him swimming up from the past as though emerging from the deep end of a pool, gasping and blinking, into the open air. The letters aren't dated, so I can't know precisely when they were written, but I'm willing to bet it was very near the time of his death. They have that feeling to me, the feeling of elegy, as though he were unsticking himself from the present and material world.

As I read the letters through the first time, I started to shake, a faint trembling that made the pages I held rustle like dry leaves. My knees and ankles, too, felt boneless. I ended up crouched on the floor by Rachel's bed.

It was a kind of furor, I suppose, a mixture of grief and incomprehension. I counted the written pages. Twelve. Twelve bound pages covered in my father's handwriting, some only half filled, some written on front and back, the words on one side seeping into the words on the other. Something about those physical pages, stapled to a light blue cover that my father had left blank, drove home to me more than anything else that he was dead. I mean, not that he was dead precisely, not in the ashes-to-ashes sense, which of course I knew, but in a fuller, more comprehensive way—that he had once been alive, young even, inhabiting the earth, sentient and sentimental, scared, tender, brave, desiring—and now he was no longer.

For days I felt nothing but exhaustion, the tiredness that comes from excavating heavy earth. Then came spikes of fury—what deprivation it seemed, my mother, my father, and me—our lives together, jostling elbows as though we were strangers on a train. I read the letters so many times I memorized parts of them. Each time I felt something different.

What I've come to feel is something akin to déjà vu. It makes me believe on some level that my father's history was imprinted on my DNA, a pattern in code snaking through my cells, as though I'd known him all along, had been carrying the whole of him within me without knowing.

Here I am . . . trapped in the past, entangled in history, wandering like a ghost. My father had written these words, but it could have been me.

This then was my inheritance, or so I came to think of it. After all, he had written in English. This fragment of life story, this map back to the vital point of origin—in some dim way my beginning, in some dark way his end, and in the middle, a convergence.

Bad Dream

I had a tremendous headache in the night, a sort of pulsing in the temples like a series of small explosions detonating inside my brain. Louise gave me some aspirin.

Sometime later I woke to a whimpering scream. It started far away and got closer and closer, until I realized that it was rising from my own throat. I sat up. The back of my nightgown was soaked in sweat. Louise and Jerry appeared, peering in at me from the door frame.

"Isa, are you okay?" Jerry asked.

I nodded slowly.

"You must have had a nightmare," said Louise. "You screamed."

"You said something," said Jerry. "It sounded like 'mean.'"

"I don't know," I said. "I don't remember."

Louise laid a palm on my forehead. "You're a little warm," she said. "Poor Isa. Try to get some sleep."

I felt my stomach buckle and turned on my side to face the wall. The moment passed. I was conscious of my breath, which sounded unnaturally loud inside my own head, labored and errant, like an old person's breathing. I strained toward the sounds of Jerry and Louise returning to bed—the twang of a mattress spring, a low cough. Dimly, in the shadows, images reasserted themselves, the vague shape of my nightmare assembling. I was conscious that I was fighting them off—these images, this shape— at the same time I willed them forward. Not a dream but a vision; not a vision but a memory; not memory but knowledge.

Dark room. Farthest part of night. Silence has a thickness, a texture. Crouched by the side of the bed. Silhouette of a figure. Tension. Holding of breath. A container pours out along the floor. Sensation of liquid, cold, stinging. Hiss of match strike. Brief scent of sulfur. Bright day and surprise. A moment of confusion, then the clarity of pain. Womanly figures dance—flailing and contorted in the eye of the flames—purple ribbons unfurling, discarding orange raiments.

Storm

It was Sunday. Outside the window, snow was falling on dead leaves. I was sitting at the kitchen table, my hands unsteady. I felt hungover, cloudy-headed. Jerry had made me tea, which had grown cold in its cup. I had had one sip and lost interest. He sat across from me, reading the newspaper, eating toast with blueberry jam.

I knew two things in that instant. That I could kill a man and that I was not a killer. Those lines kept coming back to me. I pictured my father on his knees on a grassy dune, sobbing over a boy he had just killed.

Another line returned to me. *Twice she tried to kill herself, but luckily both times I was able to prevent her.* I knew my mother had suffered after Stephen's death. She'd been hospitalized a few times, and I'd seen her, low and hollow-eyed, hunched over my brother's overalls with a pair of pinking shears. I never knew she'd attempted suicide. I tried to remember the times she went to the hospital, my father grimly stoic, guiding her to the car by her elbow, in his other hand the smallest suitcase of Black Watch plaid. My mother's expression always seemed blankest to me at these times, her beauty a mask, tight to her face, like the wig on her head covering her real hair.

How had she done it? Pills, most likely, since there'd been no scars. Or gas, maybe, in the garage before I came home from school.

I knew how she did it the time she succeeded.

Jerry looked up, as though he'd been eavesdropping on my thoughts.

"My mother did it," I said. "She set the fire."

"What?" Jerry put down his newspaper.

"I just figured it out," I said. "I found some letters . . ."

As I explained it to Jerry, I grew more convinced. My mother would have been comfortable with a burning death. She would, I was sure, have welcomed it. My mother, who believed she was a phoenix, from ashes born and borne, wondering if I'd told my father, unable to read from his expression but sensing in him a coldness, a loosing of affection; Moulten lost to her already. It was my mother who had forgotten about me. Or, maybe, who hadn't.

"*Mian* is what you heard me say in my sleep," I said. "Not me, but my mother. *Mian.* It means '*I'm sorry.*'"

We were silent for a long time after this. We sat at the

kitchen table and watched the snow. Jerry made another pot of tea and more toast. Louise came in from her morning errands, stomping the snow from the bottoms of her shoes. We told her what I suspected, and she sat, too.

"Can it make . . . ?" she said, her bowlike mouth twisting. "I mean, do you suppose it makes any difference in the end?"

"To Isa," Jerry said.

"Of course, to Isa," said Louise, as though to a child. "But, I mean, should we tell anyone else? The authorities?"

Did it make a difference? Officially? If they concluded my mother crazy instead of my father? I shrugged. "We can't prove anything."

"I can't imagine her doing it," Louise said.

"Can you imagine *him*?" Jerry asked.

Louise shook her head. "Anyone," she said.

"I can," I said. And it was true that I had imagined it one way, my father crouched in the dark, tender and unforgiving, a can of gasoline in the crook of his arm. And I'd imagined it the other, my mother overrun with grief, fumbling with a match, tears obscuring her vision. And, though in the end it was the latter image I believed, what did it really matter except that it had come down to this, for them—a dark night furiously illuminated?

We sat all day at the table, watching the unceasing blizzard, while we ourselves were indolent, mindless of time. Jerry was still in his bathrobe and pajamas, his feet in battered moccasins with holes in both toes. Louise reapplied her lipstick. The rim of her mug was stained deep red.

Eventually twilight descended, and still the snow fell, swirling in clumps and fat flakes, pink-and-blue-edged in the moon's illumination. The world had lost its definition, all its edges softening under the sculpted drift of snow, and inside the house we watched in suspended animation, as though we, too, were being muffled, soothed, covered over.

What Do You Do, Dear?

I sat with Sadie and the others on the orange shag rug in the narrow annex where Louise had her day-care center. Sadie's hair was divided into two sloppy braids. Adam sat next to her, dark and dreamy, his thumb tucked inside his mouth; on the other side was Gretchen, skinny and pale, with marbled green eyes.

"*What Do You Do, Dear?*" read Louise, holding the pink paperback high for everyone to see.

I smiled and settled back against a beanbag chair, Sadie leaning into me, her small dark head resting on my arm. I remembered reading this book to Stephen. I listened to Louise read in a silly British accent, and the children recited along with her, breathless in anticipation of the recurring punch line. *What do you do, dear?*

I looked down at Sadie and I saw Stephen. The part in her hair was crooked and white; I traced its switchbacks with my finger. It reminded me of the crack in the ceiling of our living room, the one I noticed the night my father hit me, the one I thought must go straight down to the center of the world.

I leaned closer to Sadie, smelled the earth in her hair, and I felt a tenderness like vertigo. I had to close my eyes.

It's a secondhand world we're born into. What is novel to us is only so because we're newborn, and what we cannot see, that has come before—what our parents have seen and been and done—are the hand-me-downs we begin to wear as swaddling clothes, even as we ourselves are naked. The flaw runs through us, implicating us in its imperfection even as it separates us, delivers us onto opposite sides of a chasm. It is both terribly beautiful and terribly sad, but it is, finally, the fault in the universe that gives birth to us all.

Intact

I do not know what happens next, whether I will go to college in the fall, or get a job. I'm toying with the idea of going to Korea and learning the language, maybe trying to find out what happened to my aunt. Louise thinks I should become a teacher.

The Sunday of the blizzard—the day Jerry, Louise, and I spent at the kitchen table—that was the first time I thought I might be all right.

"Come on," Jerry had said, getting up, brushing the crumbs from his lap.

"Come where?" Louise said.

"Out," he said, and took both of our hands.

"But I don't have my—" Louise protested. "Jerry! Let me at least get my—"

"Shh," he said. He slid open the door and we stepped out into the yard. The cold hit my face, and I felt the slower sensation of cold at my feet. We slogged toward where the garden had been. Louise and Jerry stopped, but I walked farther out, to the edge of the woods where the trees were hulking shapes. Snow spiraled around me, each flake seemingly phosphorescent, lit from within, as though by a tiny votive candle.

I thought of my mother's favorite Christmas decoration, the carousel of golden angels that glittered as they spun. The idea of repeated motion, of angels spinning and snow falling, seemed to elongate my sense of time, made it stretch in both directions. Inside it my parents and Stephen were alive; my aunt had never been abducted; the soldier my father had killed opened his eyes and stared out to sea.

This sense of infinite, alternate time stopped me where I stood, and I lay back in the snow. The chill made the scars on my legs pulse with a shooting pain that was itself icy cold. From where I lay, looking straight up at the sky, the snow seemed to pulse in the same rhythm. It was like witnessing the multiple birth of stars. And there in the silence, the snow, and the dark, I wept, finally, for the right reasons. Not for self-pity, or remorse, or even sadness. But in gratitude.

Acknowledgments

My gratitude to my relatives in Korea and the United States, who helped teach me the emotional history of Korea, and the enduring heart and strength that abides in its people. My father's wartime memoir was especially educational in this regard. Many thanks to my agent, Gail Hochman, for believing in me from the beginning; to Vicky Wilson, for believing in the book; and to Alice Quinn for playing literary matchmaker. To Liz Ahl, Levi Costello, John Dalton, Erin Flanagan, Hayun Jung, Robert Miller, Caroline Morris, Meg Petersen, Merryl Reichbach, Alice Staples, Zachary Wagman, and Jon Wei, for their feedback and friendship. Thanks also to Geoffrey Brock and Hayun Jung for their special contributions to this book. To the educators who inspired and encouraged me—particularly Joan Underwood,

G. Armour Craig, Mary Gordon, Marilynne Robinson, and Margot Livesey. For their gifts of time and money, I am indebted to the National Endowment for the Arts; the New Hampshire State Council on the Arts; the Millay Colony, in Austerlitz, New York; and especially to the magical MacDowell Colony in Peterborough, New Hampshire, where most of this novel was written. Thanks to my brother Kollin; Kayla and Clay, the best kids on the planet; and most importantly, to Roy Andrews, for sharing the life and the dream.

Printed in the United States
by Baker & Taylor Publisher Services